MAISY the SLAV

New York Mafia Vengeance:
Book 4

Alexandra Iff

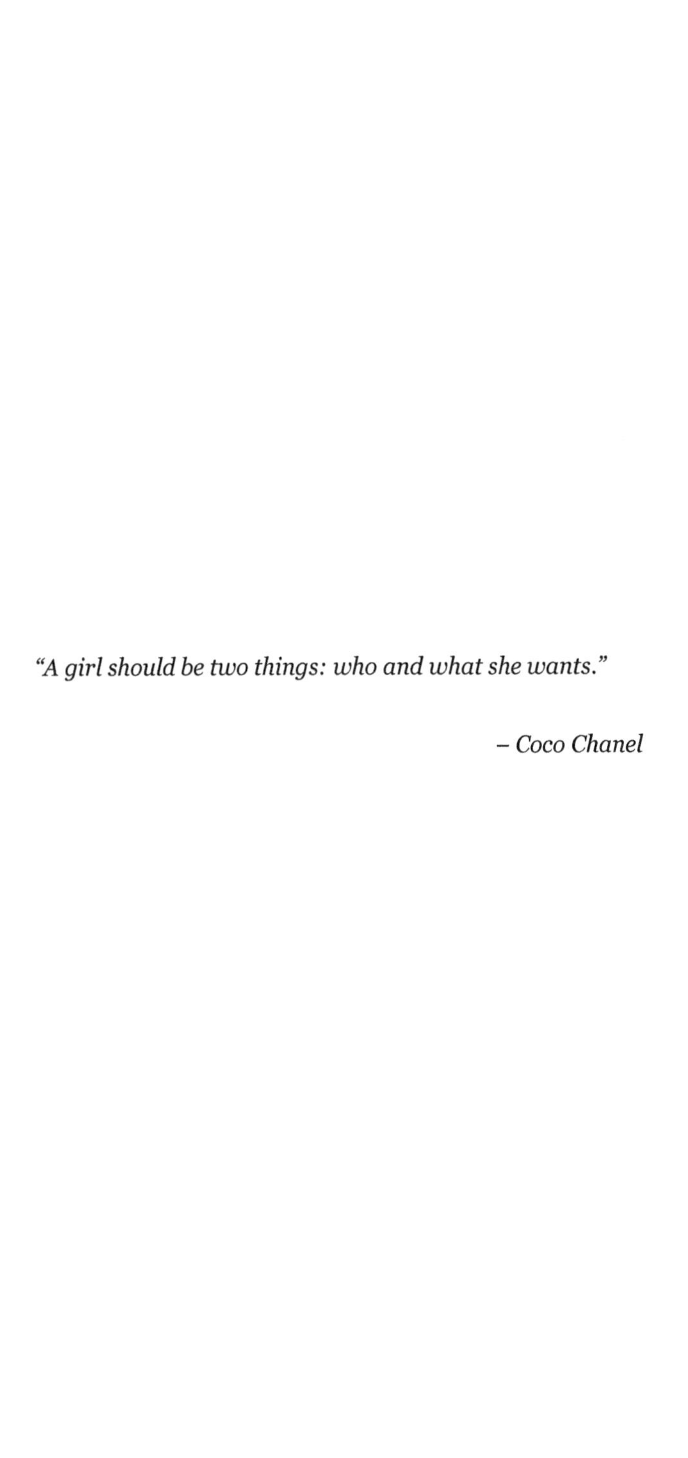

"A girl should be two things: who and what she wants."

– Coco Chanel

CONTENTS

CHAPTER 1

ORION

"She better not find out," Logan groans.

"If she does, it'll all be over," Kai says quietly, almost to himself, dragging a hand through his blond hair.

"Be clever about this," I cut in. "Go separately. One by one."

Logan lifts his head, eyes wide now. "We're actually doing this?"

"I already did," I say simply.

They both stare at me like I've just said I shot God.

Kai lets out a sharp breath. "You went to her

place?"

"Don't look at me like that," I say coolly. "It's done. And if either of you start acting like jittery schoolboys, Maisy's gonna see right through you."

"I'm not sure if I'm able to be as cool as you are, Orion." Kai shifts his weight from one foot to the other. "That lawyer shit sure comes handy in situations like these. She's gonna read me like a damn book. I can see the title now: Visiting Indra's Lair."

Logan cuts me off. "Don't say her name. You say it, and Maisy will hear it somehow."

I chuckle at their absurdity. "Come on, she's not a psychic. She may suspect. That's different."

"No, man," Logan mutters. "You don't get it. That woman's like a goddamn prophet. You lie, she smells it."

"Why the fuck are we going down this road, Orion? Isn't it easier—" Kai starts, but I cut him off.

"It's not. We talked about this; it was unanimously agreed, remember?" I stay silent until I see them nod. When they do, I continue. "Now stop being such cowards and get a grip on yourselves, men. We still rule New York. We still run everything from the courts to the docks. We've bled for this power. Don't you forget who the hell we are."

I deliver my words just like I'm in court. To the point, with power. Except I didn't count on the bedroom door creaking open. All our heads snap to the doorway. Every muscle in my body is primed in that direction, and I know it's her.

She doesn't step fully into the room, just enough for us to see the light catching her black curls. She looks innocent. Gorgeous. "Dinner's ready," she says softly. "You boys done plotting?"

We're not doing anything wrong, yet my heartbeat's a war drum now. Me, of all people. It's absurd.

Kai stands quickly, too quickly. "Hey, baby girl, just talking business. Nothing big."

Her gaze flicks to him. Stays. His shoulders twitch. "Hmm," she hums, then looks at Logan. "You okay?"

He nods slowly. "Just tired, sweetheart."

She tilts her head and smiles lazily. Dangerous. "You all smell like secrets."

"We'll join you in a moment, darling," I assure her calmly.

She lingers, narrowing her eyes at me, then turns and disappears into the hallway.

Kai's the first to speak, whisper-thin. "Told you. She knows."

MAISY

The woman in the mirror is almost a stranger: crisp white shirt, neat ponytail, not a hint of the chaos that usually clings to her, like the children's sticky fingerprints. Her turquoise cardigan adds a rebellious splash of color to her otherwise corporate armor. I catch her smiling. Two whole days of freedom stretch ahead, unmarred by juice spills and urgent cries of 'Mom!'

Having to look after six children sometimes messes with your lifestyle. Luckily, I can afford to have them taken out for a day or two with Sasha, their nanny, and a few of their bodyguards.

Of course, Sasha is not alone; she has her family joining her. They have Lisa's daughter, Mia, with them too. Mia loves the fact that she's the eldest of her cousins, and she tortures them in her own sweet way.

But I push away the familiar pang of mom guilt. Because today is an important day.

I clear my throat and enter the dining room through the back from the corridor. There is another entrance on the other side of the room through which more of my guests, all women, enter.

"Good morning."

I make my way to the head of the table, my gaze

sweeping over the room. The women murmur their greetings, each one in her own quiet way. I've braced myself for just a handful to show up, expecting embarrassment, maybe even ridicule. Instead, the eyes of around twenty women meet mine. Some are seated, others standing, all watching. No pressure.

Except, there is pressure. A lot of it. I took it upon myself to gather the wives, sisters, and girlfriends of every man in the family—whether they're a Delgado, a Vitali, or a Carte.

The reason is that I've noticed most women in the mafia world, women like me, are treated like background noise. I certainly am not. My men know my worth. From what I've seen, most women are kept on the sidelines, watching as the men handle the business.

Well, it's time we show them we can take care of New York as well.

When I shared my idea with my men, I expected hesitation—maybe even doubt. Instead, they lit up like I'd confirmed something they already knew. Logan grinned, Kai leaned back with a low whistle, and Orion—of course—smirked like he'd been waiting for that moment.

"Pay up," Orion said, extending his hand toward the other two. Logan groaned while Kai dug into his pocket, both of them chuckling.

Orion turned to me. "We had a wager on when

you'd finally make your move to do something for yourself."

I do love their support, even if it comes with smug grins and the unsettling realization that they sometimes know me better than I know myself.

"I'm grateful you all could make it," I say to my guests now, my voice steady despite the nerves. My eyes follow Lisa, Orion's sister, as she moves gracefully through the crowd, pouring coffee.

"Your email made sense, Maisy. I want in," Angelina, Uncle Colletti's daughter, begins. "You all know my husband, Adam, is a useless prick. I could easily take care of the business better than him, but my father keeps dismissing me. I think I've had enough of it."

The women around her agree noisily, and the accord spreads throughout the room.

"Absolutely, Angelina. This shouldn't be an issue in the twenty-first century," I reply. "But it's up to us to make ourselves visible."

A ripple of approval moves through the room, soft murmurs and nods of agreement. The tension in my chest eases, and just like that, my nervousness completely melts away.

"Everyone, come and sit at the table if you can. It'll be a squeeze, but we'll manage. I have a few discussions planned so we can find the right way forward. And if you have any ideas, speak up. This is our project. Our little club."

The room buzzes with energy as Leila brings in more chairs to add to the twelve already circling the table. I look around and, glancing to the side, I see Orion, his figure framed in the glass panel of the back door, watching.

"Check the table sections and sit in the one you like," I continue, determined not to get distracted.

I'm hoping they won't interfere, but just as everyone sits down and the room gets quiet, the back door opens and Orion, Logan, and Kai enter in their full glory. How they still manage to make me weak in my knees, I don't know.

Orion is in a suit, waistcoat over his shirt, his sleeves rolled up, wearing his rings and watch. Cleanshaven, hair slicked back, eyes to get lost in. I get butterflies in my stomach when he looks at me.

Logan is in his chinos, with a white coat on top. He must have gotten a call to head to the ER. He saunters toward me with a mischievous smirk that gets me every time.

And then Kai, walking behind them in only his sweatpants, his six-pack on show. His messy blond locks and his yawn tell me he's barely awake—except when my eyes drop to his crotch, I see a distension in the material that tells a story of one member that's fully awake.

Saturdays are usually lazy and lusty in our house, especially when we have the place to ourselves, but this morning, as I was getting dressed, I had to push back. I wanted to play too, but I had other things on my mind.

I look at them with a smile and tilt my head, hoping they'll understand my silent message: This better be quick.

Some of the women ogle, rather defeating the premise of women empowerment. But Lisa, as always, saves the day by distracting their attention away from us. "Ladies, do any of you have any other ideas for a group we could add to the table?"

I approach Orion and whisper sharply, "What are you doing here?"

"Can't a man miss his woman?" Orion's low voice sends a chill down my spine, even though I'm still annoyed.

I glance back around the dining room. The women are engaged in conversation, with Lisa expertly managing the different groups. Still, this isn't how I planned my morning to go.

"Logan, don't you have to go to work?" I ask, hoping he'll be the reasonable one.

"I do. Which is why I get to go first." He takes my hand and leads me out of the room, toward the staircase. I don't resist; I'm not going to make a scene. I know I'm safe. They just have some silly game in mind. Orion and Kai follow us closely, with Kai still half-asleep but somehow radiating burning heat through his sweatpants.

"First?! First what? No. Logan, I must go back," I protest, but for some reason, my feet follow his up the staircase.

"Five minutes," Logan promises with that dreamy smile that always means trouble.

The second-floor landing has a custom storage space built under the upper portion of the stairs—it's more of a hidden room, really, with a door that blends into the wall paneling. They built this space to conceal their arsenal of weapons. Orion opens it with a knowing smirk.

"In here? Are you crazy?" I yell, my pulse quickening at the thought.

"Need to remind you who's really in charge," Kai mumbles, suddenly looking more alert. I'm reminded of how they teased me earlier, saying that I'm 'taking over the family' by calling this meeting.

"Let me go!" I try to push back as they guide me into the space. "I'm only trying to empower the women, not take charge. There's a difference!"

"Right here. Bend down if you don't want us to ruin your clothes." Logan positions me at the doorframe in front of a workman's bench, the only thing that's inside. He pushes my shoulders down, but I resist.

"Logan, Kai, please. It's not the same!"

Kai's on my right, his fingers roving under my skirt and between my thighs, pulling my panties aside. As if I haven't said a word, he starts gently stroking my cunt. Fuck!

Orion is standing to my left, and rather frantically, proceeds to unbutton my shirt, pulling my breasts out of my bra while Logan shimmies my skirt up. The three of them are behind me, taking me apart in their own special way, and I already know I'm helpless. Their touch is my undoing.

"Isn't it?" Orion's voice carries that dangerous edge I know all too well. "Seems to me you're building quite the army downstairs."

"She is, isn't she? What about what we want, huh?" Kai whispers in my ear, jerking his fingers deeper inside my aroused cunt.

I struggle to think while Orion is pinching my nipples, and then sucking them, one by one. Kai's fingers go deeper, to the knuckle. I stifle a moan as they push me into the wooden bench in front of me, which digs into the tops of my thighs.

"There–you–go. Yeees..." Logan manages to fully shimmy down my panties, removing Kai's hand from between my legs, if only for a moment. With my skirt up and my panties gone, I fight to move, but only to allow more space for Kai's fingers, and those of anyone else who might have a go at me. I've lost the game, I know.

"Mmm…It's not an army. It's support. Community," I pant.

"Community?" Logan laughs as he unbuckles himself. I turn to see his cock has sprung out, glistening with a drop of precum. "Open her up," he says, and Kai's hand is right there, helping Logan by spreading my butt cheeks open as I feel the steel ridge of his erection rubbing over my wet cunt.

Orion urges me to bend over. I do, and my ass is hiked up in the air, my wet pussy open and dripping, but Logan has other ideas. He takes some of the juices from my opening and spreads them over my ass. Then he edges inside me, an inch at a time as I begin to moan. It hurts, but at the same time, I want more of him. I look back and see Orion unbuckled, fisting his cock, waiting for his turn.

Logan groans as his fingers claw into my hips and he slowly makes his way in, withdrawing and entering me again. I feel a sweet, burning pain a few more times before he's in, to the hilt. "You feel this, sweetheart?" He stops for a millisecond, then begins to pick up speed, stretching me as he takes me. "I want you to remember my cock buried deep inside you each time you want to organize a coup." Using my hips for leverage, he thrusts into me as I slowly begin to lose comprehension.

Coup?

"Fuck! Someone take over...Her sweet ass is so tight, I'm gonna cum, right...fucking...now!" He growls loudly and stills inside me, spurting his life deep within as I feel my juice dripping down my leg.

Logan pulls out and Orion steps in. "My turn! Move!"

Orion doesn't go slow or easy. He goes for my ass, balls-deep from the first stroke, with each thrust making me grunt, taking me that much closer to my own heaven, the reason why I abandoned the women downstairs.

"Yes...yes...yeees..." I whimper, my voice staccato in time with his grunts.

"Orion doesn't want you to come just yet, baby girl." Kai grins as he pumps his cock, and Logan smirks too.

"I'll see you all later. Duty calls," Logan says matter-of-factly. "And sweetheart..." He turns to me as he leaves. "Keep that cunt of yours wet for me."

Before I can say anything, Orion's hand fists my hair and pulls me to him, my back arching as far as humanly possible, baring my throat to his other hand, with which he cuts my air intake.

"Take–every–inch–of–me." He growls like an

animal, each thrust into me rough and ruthless.

Kai uses the moment to lean in from above and kiss me deep as I'm being pounded. "That's it, baby girl," he mutters against my lips as my body jerks faster and faster from Orion's thrusts. "Show us what a good little slut you are for us."

"Maisy, fuck, yes!!" Orion's hands land on my hips, drawing blood where they're digging into my flesh as he violently speeds up. I gasp out loud for air while his hot cum spurts inside me, and I hear his unmistakably guttural growl. He fills me up and then slowly pulls out, leaving me primed for Kai, who's raring to take his place.

"She's all yours, brother!" Orion steps back as Kai wraps his arm around my waist, pulls me flush to his body, and guides his cock right into my open and soaked cunt.

"Kai! Oh God, Kai!" My body responds to the pleasure as he lowers his head to my shoulder, releasing a deep groan in my ear.

"Fuck, Maisy, you feel so good."

My inner thighs are soaked with my arousal. I'm yearning for an orgasm and by God, if I don't get it, I'm going to kill someone.

"You want me, baby girl?" he whispers in my ear, holding me still as I go crazy and writhe against him, hoping he'll get the message.

"I do…Fuck me, Kai. I need it. I need you." I turn

my head and search for his lips, weaving my hand into his hair before pulling him in for a kiss. Almost instantly, he groans, and with his free hand, helps me spread my legs wider, lifting my knee onto the bench in front. He reaches between my legs, his fingers going straight for my soaked nub. I lose myself in his touch as he starts to thrust into me, harder and fiercer, knocking us against the bench with a rhythmic hammering sound.

And this is it. I know I'm going to burst. I feel it building inside me; with every thrust, I'm beginning to fly, to moan incoherently, chasing the moment that comes to me sweetly, like heaven. He pinches my swollen clit and I explode, my body jolting from the zing.

He growls as he holds me tight, making sure his cum is buried deep inside my pussy. Every last drop.

Out of breath and panting, my eyes land on Orion watching me as he fixes his cock in his pants. He probably has another hard-on.

Kai pulls out and slaps my ass, making me squeal and giggle.

"You want more, Kai?" I purr as I start fixing my skirt. It will have to do as my panties are somewhere on the floor, ruined.

Kai tugs up his sweatpants. "What I want is for you to remind me why there are so many women downstairs?"

"Women deserve a voice—" I start, but Kai

interrupts me with a wet, sweaty kiss.

"You have a voice," he murmurs, "and three men who hang on your every word."

"You're exposing yourself to risk, Maisy." Orion's voice has turned somber, and that's never a fun vibe. "I don't need to tell you that."

"I thought you liked me doing something for myself!" I put my hands on my hips. "And exactly how am I exposing myself to risk?"

"Everyone has their own agenda."

"No, they don't. All they need is someone to talk to, someone to hear them out." I feel my frustration rising, Orion's getting under my skin. "Anyway. I gotta go. They're waiting for me."

"Maisy—"

I hear Kai's voice, but ignore it as I finish buttoning up my shirt and straightening my skirt. I also attempt to fix my hair as I run down the stairs.

When I eventually return to the dining room, my hair is still a mess despite my best efforts to fix it, and I know I'm flushed. Lisa gives me a knowing look but says nothing. Luckily no one else notices, as the women are fully engaged in conversation.

CHAPTER 2

MAISY

"These women have so much potential," I say as I arrange the chairs around the massive wooden table for the day's meeting.

Lisa nods as she places cups on the table. "Angelina especially. Did you know she's been managing most of Uncle Colletti's legitimate businesses behind the scenes?"

"Really?" This catches my attention. "For how long?"

"Years. But her father insists everything goes through Adam. He thinks their conversations are no place for a woman."

I shake my head, thinking of Angelina's

husband. "That's exactly what we need to change. Not by fighting the men, but by showing them what we can bring to the table."

"Speaking of bringing things to the table," Lisa says, "Celina approached me after the last meeting. She wants to train some of us in self-defense."

"The jujitsu expert from Carte security? That's perfect!" I pause, considering the implications. "But we'll need to present it carefully. Some of the men may feel their masculinity's being challenged."

"I'll bet," Lisa agrees.

"As long as they know we're trying to contribute, not take over, they should be fine." I arrange the name cards, grouping women with complementary skills together.

Lisa picks up one of the cards. "You know what impressed me most about the first meeting? How many of these women already have skills and connections we didn't know about. Like Gizelle running that import business through her cousins in Italy."

"Or Georgina's network in real estate," I add. "We've been sitting on all this untapped potential."

"Our men aren't stupid," Lisa points out, and starts helping me set up the coffee station. "They must know what their wives and daughters are capable of."

"They know. But old habits die hard. Change is scary, and dangerous, especially in our world." I check the time, then notice Lisa's eyes are fixed on me.

"You seem calmer than last time," she observes.

"I am. I'm glad I'm doing this." I straighten up a crooked place setting.

"You're a good leader. I know your men think that."

"Oh, stop it, Lisa. You're just gonna make me blush." I pause, my thoughts drifting to Orion, Logan, and Kai.

Their behavior lately has been confusing. They always let me in on the intelligence about any deals or troubles the family might have, but a few times now I've sensed they were keeping something to themselves.

And so, instead of coming clean, they've started playing their own games. Each of them has played with me on their own, which is not unusual, but the way they're doing it, I'm certain something's off.

Orion caught up with me first, last Monday morning, while I was sorting laundry in the utility room.

"Still feeling in charge?" he asked me, his voice making me jump and drop the sheet I was folding.

"I'm always in charge of laundry," I replied, trying to keep my voice steady. "Unless you'd like to take over?"

He just smiled that dangerous smile of his. "Oh, I can think of better things to take over."

What followed was definitely not about laundry.

Or me being in charge in any way.

On Tuesday afternoon, it was Logan who found me in the kitchen as I was planning meals for the week.

"Making executive decisions about dinner?" he drawled, coming up behind me.

"Someone has to feed this army," I smiled, trying to focus on my list even as his proximity sent my thoughts scattering.

"Speaking of armies..." He turned me around to face him. "How's your recruitment going?"

That conversation ended with the grocery list forgotten on the counter.

Kai's turn came on Wednesday. I was organizing the playroom when he appeared, leaning against the doorframe with a grin that spelled trouble.

"Playing general, even with the toys?" he teased.

I gestured at the chaos of stuffed animals and building blocks. "Everything needs structure."

"Structure?" He chuckled and moved closer. "Is that what you need?"

Needless to say, the toys stayed unorganized.

The memories of the past week make me blush, even now as I set up the room with Lisa.

Between these encounters, we've had conversations about the women's club and my intentions with it. What I am going to do with it.

However, not one conversation has been about

what the three of them are doing. What the three of them are hiding from me.

"Earth to Maisy." Lisa's voice pulls me back to the present. "Where did you go just now?"

"Just thinking about how supportive everyone's been," I say diplomatically.

Her knowing smirk tells me she's not fooled. "Uh-huh. Is that why you're blushing?"

"Focus on the setup," I deflect, but can't help grinning.

The crunch of tires on gravel makes us both snap to attention. Cars are already pulling up. "Early arrivals. You ready?"

"Always." Lisa gives the room a final scan. "What are we doing today?"

"Building trust. Getting them to open up about their skills, their ideas. If we want men to take us seriously, we need to take ourselves seriously first."

"And Celina's self-defense classes?"

"We'll present it as a security measure. The more capable everyone is, the safer all our families are."

The front door opens, and voices flood the hallway. Lisa squeezes my hand before going to greet our guests.

I take a deep breath, centering myself. Last week was about bringing these women together. This week is about showing them who we can become. Not a separate force within the families, but an integral part of making our world stronger, and more secure.

The dining room starts to fill, and I see the change already. Women who barely spoke last week are greeting each other like old friends. They're networking, sharing ideas, building connections.

This is what I wanted. A step into a new era. One where everyone's seen and heard.

I clear my throat, ready to begin the second meeting.

ORION

Blood and bedtime stories. That's my life now.

I watch from the doorway as controlled chaos unfolds. Earlier today, I ordered a hit on a rival faction from Chicago. Now I'm monitoring the construction of a pillow fortress. The duality would be amusing if it wasn't so goddamn precarious.

Maxim and Luca are the architects, their little faces serious as they stack cushions. Five and four years old, and already showing signs of the men they'll become. Maxim plans; Luca executes. Just like their fathers.

Mila, our three-year-old hurricane, "helps" by systematically dismantling their work. She's just like Kai in her determination. Damien toddles after them all, observing with the same quiet intensity as Logan has.

The twins, Ava and Grace, babble in their playpen. One year old and already plotting, their expressions look just like Maisy's. I make a mental note to upgrade our security again. Six children. Seven including Mia. Seven potential targets.

Maisy sits cross-legged on the floor, simultaneously supervising and preventing Damien from eating the art supplies. She laughs, low and easy, and all I can think of is how much I love her.

"Fort looking good, boys," Logan says, entering with bottles for the twins. His hospital ID still hangs from his pocket, emergency surgeon by day, mafia head by night. The perfect cover.

Kai sprawls on what's left of the couch, fresh from a "boxing match" that was really an arms deal. He scoops Mila up in his arms. "Princess, let your brothers build for five minutes before destroying their work."

"No," she replies, a frown on her tiny face.

I check my phone: confirmation of the hit. Clean. Professional. I tuck it away as Maxim calls, "Daddy, look!"

"Very impressive," I say, but my attention is on

Maisy. She's in her element—drawing everyone in, commanding the room without even trying.

"You're thinking too loud," Logan murmurs beside me.

He's right. I'm always thinking. Planning. Seven children mean seven vulnerabilities.

"Bath time in ten," Maisy announces.

The protests are immediate. I notice how Kai's hand instinctively moves toward his concealed weapon at the sudden noise. We're all still adapting to domestic life.

I move to help Maisy up, pulling her flush against me. "Are you happy?" I ask quietly.

"You know I am," she purrs.

"Just be careful," I murmur, brushing a kiss against her lips.

Logan steps in, wrapping his arms around Maisy's waist from behind. "We just want you safe," he says.

"I am safe," she smiles. "I have you three."

Kai appears with a twin in each arm. "You do, but these meetings of yours—"

"Are necessary," she interrupts, "and you know it."

She's right. The families need to evolve. But her growing influence is making waves. Creating attention.

My phone buzzes—another business matter.

Later. Right now, it's time for bedtime stories.

The next hour follows our carefully choreographed routine. Baths supervised in shifts, toys scooped from sudsy water, stories read while little heads lean heavy against shoulders. And finally, bedtime kisses and quiet goodnights.

When all the children are finally asleep, we gather in the living room.

The house is secure, and for a moment, we're just a normal family.

"They're getting louder," Maisy says, curled up against Kai. "The women. They want to be heard."

"They want power," I correct.

"Is that so wrong? You three share power."

Sitting on the other side of her, Logan runs a hand through her hair. "It's different with us."

She doesn't understand that every person she brings into our circle is another potential threat. Another variable. Another weakness.

But she's also right.

My phone buzzes again. For now, I silence it. Tonight is for family. For figuring out how to evolve without exposing our throat.

CHAPTER 3

MAISY

Angelina's knuckles are white where her fingers grip her coffee cup. Not a good sign.

"They laughed at us," she spits out. "Actually laughed."

Beside her, Celina sits ramrod straight with rage in her eyes.

"Tell me everything," I say, watching Lisa pour more coffee. Our dining room feels too small for all this fury.

"We presented the security initiative to Uncle Colletti," Celina begins. "Simple stuff—training the women in basic self-defense, teaching them to spot surveillance. Things that could save their lives."

"Essential skills," I agree, remembering how those same skills once saved me from one of Milan's men. Back when I was still searching for Rosey.

"My father called it cute," Angelina cuts in, voice dripping with venom. "Said we should focus on planning the next family dinner instead. Like we're still living in the 1950s."

"Then Adam started in," Celina continues, her fingers drumming a deadly rhythm on the table. "Said women shouldn't worry their pretty heads about security. That's when I almost showed him exactly what these pretty hands can do."

"What stopped you?" Lisa asks, settling into the chair beside me.

"Uncle Leo." Angelina's lip curls. "Walked in, took one look at the situation, and said—what was it exactly, Cel?"

Celina mimics his condescending tone perfectly. "Ladies, why create problems where there are none? Our security is impeccable."

I grip my cup tighter. "The Martinez widow probably thought her security was impeccable, too."

Silence falls. We all remember how that ended— Maria Martinez, gunned down in her own driveway. No training. No awareness. No chance. Clueless as to how to protect herself. And the thing is, they weren't even going after her.

"It got worse after that," Angelina continues. "We brought up the Martinez case, and my father—" her voice catches. "He said if I had time to worry about security, maybe I wasn't spending enough time with my husband."

"They're scared," Lisa observes quietly. "Change threatens them."

"They should be more scared of leaving us vulnerable," Angelina concludes.

"We're seen as the weak link." Celina stands, clearly needing to move. "The easy target."

"I tried explaining the benefits," Angelina says. "How trained women could spot surveillance, identify threats. You know what Uncle Leo said?"

"Something infuriating, I'm sure," Lisa mutters.

Angelina's laugh is hollow. "Stick to the kitchen, let the men handle danger."

I pace the length of the dining room, my mind racing. "We need a different approach."

"They won't listen to us," Celina says. "No matter how logical the argument."

"Then we make them listen. By using the men who do take us seriously."

"My brother, Logan, and Kai." Lisa nods. "They have influence. Heck, they're the heads of the syndicate."

"More than influence," I correct. "They have

vision. They understand that strong women make stronger families."

LOGAN

Lately, I've found myself paying closer attention to the details around me, noticing things I might have overlooked before. And right now, I'm noticing how Maisy stabs her pasta with more force than necessary. We're at the dinner table, winding down after a hard day's work. Kai and I have no problem being at home in sweatpants and t-shirts, but Orion's still in his three-piece suit.

Leila moves silently around us, refilling wine glasses. Maxim and Luca are engaged in their usual dinner competition of who can eat the slowest, while Mila creates abstract art with her ketchup. The twins, mercifully, are focused on their bottles, and Damien...well, more food is on him than in him.

"They laughed at them," Maisy says suddenly, her voice tight. "Actually laughed."

Orion sets down his fork. "Colletti's always been traditional."

"Traditional?" she scoffs. "Try medieval."

"Mama, what's medieval?" Maxim asks.

"It means very old-fashioned, buddy," Kai answers, smoothly intercepting a spoonful of pasta that Mila aims at Luca.

I catch Maisy's eye across the table. "Tell us exactly what happened."

Maisy launches into the story, each sentence laced with frustration as she recounts what went down.

"Ava, no throwing," Orion interrupts Maisy, then continues. "Colletti's resistance isn't surprising. Change threatens him."

"It shouldn't," Maisy argues. "Strong women make stronger families."

"We know that," I say, wiping Damien's face, "but they see any change as a loss of control."

"Then they're idiots."

"Mama said a bad word!" Mila announces gleefully.

"Inside voice, princess," Kai reminds her, but I catch him smiling. "And yes, they're idiots."

Orion leans forward. "You know, we can talk to them. But—"

"I know you can." She's almost too confident.

Orion nods at me, then at Kai—silent but clear. It's time.

"But right now, darling, we want to talk to you

about something else. About next weekend."

Maisy frowns. "What about next weekend?"

Kai chuckles. "We have a little surprise for you."

"A surprise?" Her brows hitch.

"Is it your birthday, Mommy?" Mila asks.

"It's not, honey." Maisy looks suspiciously at the three of us. "I don't know what your dads are talking about. I have the club meeting—"

"Which can be rescheduled," Orion cuts in smoothly. "We need you with us."

"You need me, or you have a surprise for me? Which is it?"

I smirk at her. "The first one is always valid. And we do have a surprise for you. So, both."

"Daddy, can I have juice?" Maxim interrupts.

"Finish your water first," Orion says without looking away from Maisy. "So?"

"You're not being fair," she breathes.

"Think of it as prioritizing," I try to explain.

I note the signs of her internal struggle; we haven't had a surprise for her since, well, ever. We take her to dinner, and she loves the theatre and the ballet, so we go there, but she's never had a proper surprise. What she has coming to her will blow her mind. It took us a lot to pull this together without her knowing, and for that, she's going to have to cancel her meeting. Definitely.

"Fine," she finally says. "But this better be worth

it."

"Oh, it will be," Orion promises, his voice dropping lower.

"Papa, you're using your scary voice," Mila observes.

We all laugh and I see Maisy's mood lighten as her shoulders ease, just a fraction. A small sign, but it's enough. She's allowing us to take care of her again.

"Leila," I call, "the children might want their dessert in the playroom tonight. Can you manage by yourself?"

Our housekeeper moves efficiently, gathering plates and children with practiced ease. "Sure," she states matter-of-factly.

"I called Sasha, she should be here soon. She'll be helping you put the children to bed," Orion informs her, ignoring Maisy's eyes burning into him. Good man. He's always ten steps ahead.

Leila leaves the dining room, and then it's just us adults.

"So," Maisy says once we're alone, "You said you can help. Tell me about your strategy for handling Colletti."

"In the morning," Orion promises. "Right now, I wanna do something else with you."

Her breath catches. "The children—"

"Are well supervised," Kai finishes.

I stand, moving behind her chair. My hands find her shoulders, feeling the tension there. "You need to unwind. Doctor's orders."

"Are you sure it's a good idea?" she purrs.

Orion chuckles. "Sex is always a good idea."

"Come on." Kai stands up. "Unless you'd rather discuss family politics?"

She rises from her chair and locks eyes with me, then with Orion, then Kai. An infinitesimal smile shows on her lips and she heads toward the stairs.

The three of us follow close behind, like men under a spell—helpless, willing, and completely hers.

KAI

"I need a shower," Maisy sighs, peeling her dress up and over her head in one fluid motion. Wearing only panties, she steals my breath.

"Hurry up, sweetheart." Logan takes off his top and lies down on our bed in his sweatpants, while Orion takes his time with his suit, methodical and controlled, slowly working each button.

"I'll help her." I press my palm to the small of

her back, guiding her toward the bathroom. It's a pointless gesture—this is her house too—but she lets me have this moment of pretending I'm in charge.

"I guess it's you and me in here, Kai," she purrs.

I follow her into the bathroom; she halts at the mirror, and our eyes meet in the reflection. There's a softness in her gaze—disarming, almost dangerous in the way it unravels something in me.

I chuckle and move a strand of her hair from her shoulder, and kiss her slowly. Standing behind her, I kiss her back, moving down her spine, going lower until I kneel and pull her panties down. I kiss her butt cheeks, then tap her on the leg, and she lifts one foot and then the other to allow me to take her panties off.

I take her hand and guide her behind the glass door as I run the shower. The water sprays and soaks me too, but I don't mind. I kiss her softly, chastely on the lips, moaning into her kiss, then step out to take off my wet clothes. My cock is hard as steel, and I know I've been controlling myself for too long.

"You're beautiful, baby girl."

She smiles and tilts her head back, her eyes closed, her face and hair enveloped by the flow of water, steam slowly filling the stall.

"My cock can't wait," I whisper in her ear as I grab her neck from behind, push her against the wall and press my body flat against hers. I rub myself against her, moving my hips back and forth.

She moans as I sink my teeth into her shoulder, hard enough to leave marks. I hear her whimper. "Kai..."

Her legs open for me; her ass perks up. I can tell how horny she's getting as I hold her tight, pressing her body against the wall and rubbing my cock between her butt cheeks.

"I know, baby girl, I can feel how much you want me," I murmur before sucking on her earlobe. She shudders and pushes her ass into me.

I wrap my hand around her wet hair and yank her head back, exposing her neck to me. She bends backward and I latch onto her nipples, sucking and biting one at a time.

Then I kiss her, weaving my tongue into her mouth and drawing a long moan out of her.

"Show me what this mouth can do, Maisy." I spin her to face me before forcing her descent, watching her gracefully sink to her knees. I take her wet hair again, one thick lock in each hand, and hold her face steady as my cock hits her face.

"Say aaah."

No complaints from her. She wants this, I know. She opens up, and when she takes my cock in her mouth, I nearly pass out from the sweet pleasure. I don't want this moment to end. "That's right, baby girl. Now, look up at me." She gazes up into my eyes, her head bobbing as I pull her hair, making sure she does a good job. Our eyes are locked and the view I have is one to die for. I'm not going to last long, that's for sure.

"Fuck, Maisy, what you're doing to me..." The deeper she takes me, with the gurgling sounds she makes, the louder I grunt. I'm so close that I tighten my fingers in her hair, quickening the pace. After a good, sweet while of face fucking, I can't avoid the inevitable any longer. My grunts change into one long growl, and my hot cum shoots to the back of her throat.

She swallows, gulping down every last drop. All the while, our eyes remain locked. Fuck, this woman is God-sent.

As if he was waiting at the door, Orion shows up in his boxer shorts. "What's taking so long?"

I smirk and turn the shower off. "Maisy's shower took a little longer than planned."

Maisy grins as she stands up and wipes the side of her mouth, but Orion clearly doesn't find it funny. He's too intense sometimes.

"We had a head start, Kai and I," Maisy purrs.

CHAPTER 4

MAISY

"Move," Orion commands, creating just enough space for Kai to slip past.

Kai smirks and presses his lips to mine, which are still pulsating from my wicked activities only moments ago. "Looking forward to seeing what the rest of the night brings," he murmurs, and I giggle. He makes me feel like a teenager.

The moment Kai's gone, the atmosphere shifts like a storm is coming—heavy, electric. Orion's fingers dig into my wrist as he yanks me with him.

"Come on, darling. We want to see our little whore in her full glory."

I writhe against his iron grip, but I know better

than to rebel. This is just foreplay to him. With Orion, sex isn't just pleasure—it's warfare.

He twists my arm behind my back and drags me out of the bathroom like a criminal. Water is dripping everywhere.

"Get ready to pump this whore tonight, boys."

Just as he says that, I manage to set myself free and start running across the room. Kai is lying on the bed, naked, Logan propped up on a pillow beside him— both watching me like predators amused by their prey.

Orion's eyes glint with a special dark hue; I can tell he's annoyed because this is so not under control. Also, he's dangerously aroused.

In one large stride, he catches up to me, tosses me onto the bed next to Logan, and holds me down with his knee as I scream and laugh. He opens the bedside drawer and retrieves a pair of metal handcuffs from the secret compartment in there, where we keep the rest of our toys. In a second, he's on top of me, straddling me.

"No, stop it, don't!" I hiss. "What if the kids come in?" I try to appeal to his conscience, but we all know the door to this bedroom has a latch, for this reason exactly.

"You running away is gonna cost you," he huffs, "a lot." His breath is labored yet he's still stronger, managing to cuff my left hand to the bedpost above my head. "It's only fair." He takes my other hand but I resist, using all my strength in my attempts to set myself free. "Besides, now you have a safe word." He finally bests me and secures my other wrist, cuffing me to the bedframe, then slaps my inner thigh. "Use it, slut!"

I'm wet; I have a craving deep in my groin, and I've been horny since I sucked Kai's cock and now I'm tied to the bed, without the power to do anything about it.

"Orion!" I yell and lunge at him, hoping to bite him, but he speedily ducks away, saving himself from my jaws. He grabs me by the neck and slams my head down on the bed.

"Yeah? You mad? Tell me how much!"

Forced down, I'm getting crazier by the second as he comes close to my lips. He's choking me with his hand, and I also feel his teeth on my cheek now; I turn to him, hoping to nip something, but he only strengthens his grip.

"I don't hear you screaming your safe word, Maisy, so I take it you must like this." He laughs. "Or maybe you've forgotten it?"

With the smirk still on his face and his hand firmly pressing on my neck, he leans closer and nips at my cheek. Each successive nibble gets closer to my lips and I turn toward him, waiting for the moment our lips meet. Upon reaching me, he kisses me, and I lunge at him full-on, weaving my tongue inside his mouth. Our teeth nearly clash with the force, but it's too short. He pulls back as I follow him, lifting my head as far as I can, my lips parted and that ache in my groin reminding me of the fact that I need him. Need them.

"Last chance for your safe word," he whispers.

I gaze at him with my mouth open, my lips wet. "I need you," I breathe. I want them tonight.

He slides his hand between my thighs and everything in my mind clears as my focus zooms in on my cunt. I breathe and wait for his fingers to do their magic. He pushes his middle and ring finger inside me slowly, taking my arousal with him, and slides them over my swollen nub as I moan. My hips sway against his hand. I need friction, more friction, but he has other ideas.

With his cock hard and eyes full of fire, he straddles me high, above my breasts. "And I need you, my whore."

Making sure he's not pressing on my chest, he moves high enough to slap me on my face with his erection. I try to move out of the way; his girthy cock is not gonna harm me, but his piercing could potentially chip my teeth if I'm not careful.

"Open wide."

I open, happy to take his cock in, and I start sucking like I've been denied it for years. He's given me a crumb of hope, shown me the light, and that's where I'm heading. His hand is no longer on my pussy but supporting my head as he begins fucking my mouth.

"Sweetheart, don't forget me." Logan's words have perfect timing, because I'm losing myself in the craving. He positions himself behind Orion and grips my inner thighs.

"Sweet Jesus mama! You're dripping."

He pushes my legs open and blows on me, teasing. Muffled sounds escape my mouth as I bob my head. Loud moans make the back of my throat vibrate. I need Logan to fuck me, or eat me, anything! And then, in an instant, I'm there. He forcefully latches onto my clit and starts sucking me, fucking me with his tongue as deep as he can go. His hands squeeze my breasts and pinch my nipples, hard. He laps at my juices and grazes my clit with his teeth. His tongue does wonders, and I ride the waves of pleasure taking me high and crashing me down, all the while moaning around Orion's cock. My body's shaking from the imminent rapture.

"Fuck! You're gonna make me—" Orion grunts. The sound morphs into a long growl, and he spurts rope after rope into my mouth. I feel the warm liquid at the back of my throat, and I keep swallowing.

"That was one fucking show!" Kai snickers as he pumps his cock leisurely, now hard again, the precum shining at the tip.

I can't help the victorious curl of my lips as I

close my eyes, feeling the relief of Orion climbing off and lying by my side. "You can untie me now, Orion," I purr.

"Untie you? We've just started playing, slut," he taunts.

I don't know what it is about those filthy words, or the way he says them, but the renewed heat between my legs is instantaneous.

Logan sits up and takes his sweatpants off, then his boxers, revealing his huge hard-on. The bedside drawer is opened again and he pulls out the leather ankle cuffs, the ones that are connected with a chain. "I wanna try something, sweetheart."

"Come on, Logan, untie me. I wanna be able to touch you..." I object, but he takes my left ankle, fixes the leather restraint to it, then does the same with my right ankle. My legs are now restricted to probably twenty inches apart. "Logan, please! This—This makes me..."

He smirks. "Horny? Wanton? Slutty? A bigger whore than you already are?"

He secures the chain from my ankle cuffs with another one from the top of our bedframe, pulling my legs up and coiling me fully like a pretzel, with my ass and cunt up in the air.

"There you go." He slaps my thighs and looks at Kai. "What do you think?"

"Perfect! You going first, or shall I?"

"The doctor must check first if everything is

okay." Logan's fingers trace my cheekbone with deceptive tenderness, brushing aside a wayward strand of hair stuck to my face. "Isn't that right, sweetheart?"

I nod, and he starts rubbing my cunt with his cock, smearing my arousal over my opening, working my slit up and down. I moan in pleasure and frustration. Being tied up is seriously messing with my head. Logan's sitting with his knees spread open in front my pussy, he pumps his cock, showing off his defined biceps, then holds it there, at my entrance, now soaked. He raises his hips and continues to rub his cock against me, dipping inside but only a little, teasing me into oblivion.

"D-Doctor?" I ask, half-moaning, half-panting. I'm getting lightheaded from the want. I need him inside me and I'm going crazy from the torment. "Is everything okay down there, doctor?"

"Yes, you're perfect, sweetheart." He pushes his hard, thick cock inside me and growls, overwhelming me with his size and girth, then pulls out again, making me lose my mind. Before I can moan my frustration he's in again, the sheer pleasure rendering me speechless. Then he starts slowly thrusting, to the hilt and out again. The position I'm in helps him enter me fully and God, it's so good. I groan with each thrust.

I hear Kai's voice in the background. "Fuck, Logan, I need her."

Logan pulls out, slaps my thigh, and makes

space for Kai, who's way too eager, already with his stealthy rod in his hand, his fingers curled around the glans. He doesn't wait, just enters me rough, hard.

"Fuck yes, so tight!" Kai starts fucking me, and it takes me a moment to adjust to his big cock. "This pussy's gonna be stretched by the time we're done with you."

I'm contorted in a strange way and all my senses are homed in on my cunt. But he plays with me, pulling out and slamming inside me again.

"P-Please...I want to..." I beg.

"What, baby girl? To cum?" he teases.

Logan stands next to the bed, turns my face sideways and finds my mouth. He gives me something else to focus on: his cock. I moan eagerly and open without him having to ask. I start licking his cock like it's a popsicle. It gets my mind off the torment Kai's putting me through.

"Thaaat's it, you're doing so good, sweetheart," Logan mutters.

"Kai, pull out," Orion calls to Kai, who obeys without hesitation. Lying next to me on the bed, Orion lifts my hips in his arms and scoots his body under my ass—his crotch area, to be precise. I try to see what's happening, but Logan's in front of me, his veiny cock deep in my throat. Being cuffed with my arms and legs above my head makes it hard for me to do anything.

"Don't worry, Maisy, the doctor's gonna take good care of you." Logan seems to sense my panic and pushes my head onto his cock, throat-deep, and after a few hard thrusts, my air supply is cut off by the size of him. I gurgle and fight for oxygen while he lets out a long groan, clearly enjoying me like this, helpless. "Thaaat's right my sweetheart, you'll be fine."

My eyes are popping out of my head, and I'm just about to turn my head away when he pulls out, giving me a second to gulp down as much air as I can. Then, he's back in my throat, his pace increased, slamming into me. "That's it, that's it, sweetheart. Good girl."

The world is becoming distant. I become aware of the sensation of being rimmed. My ass reacts to Orion's cock between my buttocks. He slides it over my arousal a few times, and slowly, after a few tries, he forces himself into my ass. I let out a stifled moan, Logan's cock still in my mouth, and feel Orion holding my hips firmly in place as he begins to pound my ass. Kai's cock slides over my cunt, looking for a way to enter me again, and he does. My arousal helps too, and I start flying. My whole being is transported to another dimension. Every hole filled. I'm there again, gliding in the space of only nerve endings and nothing else. Orion and Kai pump my body, driving in and out.

Kai growls and pistons harder each time into my

cunt, while Orion slams his cock into my ass and Logan fucks my mouth. Their grunting is my undoing. I'm asphyxiated, in a flying frenzy as orgasmic waves toss me around, crashing over my body. I'm given air again, enough to warn them of my ensuing storm.

"Kai…Logan…Orion…" My body undulates with them.

Logan, always thinking of my well-being, releases the chain that was holding my legs above my head, my arms too, but continues to face-fuck me. My legs rest on Kai's shoulders as his speed increases, his cock getting firmer with each thrust. Together with Orion, they're taking my whole body for a ride, and I have no thought process any longer.

"Look at this little slut we're fucking," Orion pants.

"She's so pretty!" Kai growls and speeds up with his feral pounding.

Someone touches my swollen nub, and that is it for me. I explode. I writhe and buck, taking Logan with me too. He groans and pulls his cock out of my mouth, shooting rope after rope over my face as I hold my tongue out.

Kai explodes with a roar, his hot cum spurting inside me as my body burns. Riding my waves high, I keep bucking into Orion's thrusts, milking him too as he pinches my nipples and then claws at my hips. He stills inside of me with a grunt, emptying his seed into my ass.

Exhausted, Logan sprawls next to Orion on the bed and Kai does the same, his breath ragged and fast, sweat clinging to his skin. I'm still lying on top of Orion, totally spent, the four of us breathless.

I grin. "You boys sure know how to help me unwind."

Their mingled laughter is heaven and hell combined.

"Saturday. Be ready at ten," Orion states, his tone leaving no room for argument.

"What's my surprise?" They are serious about this. Suddenly, I'm excited like a small child.

"Wear heels. I like you in heels." Logan's words are a command, not a suggestion.

"Heels? I—"

"Baby girl," Kai interrupts, "you know better than to argue."

Kai usually takes my side...

"Okay. Sure." I slowly move to pull Orion's cock from my ass and he groans. I lie on the bed between him and Logan, then turn to Orion and wrap my arms around him. "See? This is how I wanted to touch you, and you didn't let me." I fake a pout.

"But would you have as good an orgasm if you weren't cuffed?" Orion chuckles.

Logan shakes his head. "I doubt it."

CHAPTER 5

ORION

I'm trying to focus on the sun rising over Manhattan, but Logan's damn pacing around the room is driving me crazy. I glance over at Kai, who's sprawled in his chair and looking deceptively relaxed.

We're in Logan's penthouse, our new headquarters. Being so high up, we've learned, has its advantages. We can see a lot of things from up here and solve many problems.

Except this one, it seems. We've been up since dawn, doing the last preparations with some uncertainty. The three of us even dressed properly, Kai included. Dressed like this, we look like we're going to a wedding or a funeral.

The weight of what's at stake bears down on me like a loaded gun.

We've talked about this for quite some time before coming to a unanimous decision. But it wasn't easy. We still don't know how she will react. All we know is that we love her and would give our lives for her. That has never changed.

But there is a small chance that our action could be misinterpreted. Still, if she agrees, it will solve the only problem we may come across in our lives. We haven't yet, and I doubt we ever will, but with me being me, wanting to keep everything under control and without any margin for error, I want this sorted too.

I glance at my desk again. Three rings sit on it. Three promises. Three ways this could all go terribly wrong.

"She might think we're only after her share of New York," Logan says.

"She won't," Kai argues.

I'm twisting one of my own rings agitatedly, the metal warm from the constant friction. "If she does, maybe we don't know her at all."

The three of us have barely left Logan's penthouse this past week, planning and plotting, but one thought still stalks me: what if she hates the idea?

"This is the only way forward. Making it official,"

I reaffirm to myself. "Four families, one union."

Logan narrows his eyes. "You really think they'll accept it? Three men marrying one woman?"

I smile coldly. "They'll accept what we tell them to accept."

"Fuck yeah they will." Kai grins wickedly.

"But what if Maisy—" Logan starts.

"Maisy needs to choose it," I finish. "Freely."

Because that's the crux of it. We can force the families to accept our decision. We can't—won't—force her.

"She loves us," Kai says with certainty. "She's gonna be over the moon."

I stand, moving to the window. Below, New York pulses with life and death, power and submission. Our domain.

The rings catch the light. They're like us—three dark forces circling a brilliant star. We had them custom-made at Indra's, the jeweler next to the Four Seasons Hotel, at very short notice. It was a real mission keeping it from Maisy. We couldn't go together, not without raising suspicion, so each of us went separately—me first, then Logan, then Kai—each slipping away with some excuse, each designing it with Indra like it was our deepest secret.

It wasn't just about the rings. It was about getting it right. The weight, the design—something that would say what we think every day: you're ours, and we are yours.

Platinum, palladium, and gold. All three rings have a single black diamond and slot together into a trinity ring, a design that features three diamonds set side by side on the band.

Logan runs a hand through his hair. "She'll question everything. The logistics, the legalities…"

"Let her," I drawl. "I have answers."

"She'll worry about the children," Kai reminds us.

"They're already ours," I counter. "Papers would just make it official."

"It's time." Logan checks his watch. "Emilio should be waiting for us downstairs."

MAISY

I've racked my brain trying to figure out what the surprise could be, and for the life of me, I've got nothing. The three of them have been acting a little off around the house—whispering, exchanging looks—but nothing has set off any real alarm bells.

Emilio has just brought me to the penthouse and I'm still in the car, waiting, when the door swings open and Kai slides in, wearing a suit. Kai's wearing a suit?

He leans over, kisses me softly on the lips, and grins. "Hey, baby girl. You look gorgeous in red."

"Thank you, Kai," I purr. I know the red bodycon dress I have on fits me like a glove. "You don't look bad yourself."

Logan gets in and kisses my cheek as he sits down. "Thank you for wearing the heels, I adore you in them," he whispers in my ear. He fixes his crotch, and I feel my skin flushing pink.

Orion sits next to me, gently placing his hand on my knee. As he leans in to give me a kiss, the hand slides under my dress and between my thighs. He's going straight for my honey pot, flooding my entire body with heat and desire.

"Hey." I take away his hand, not allowing him to see if I'm wearing panties or not. I'm not. Besides, Emilio is in the driver's seat. We won't be doing any of that right now, that's for sure.

"What's going on with all of you? Since when do you wear a three-piece suit, Kai? Something's different."

"Why? Don't we look good?" Logan teases.

"No. You look too good. Like you're ready for something."

Kai grins. "Maybe we are."

"Hmm. You're definitely up to something."

"We told you we have a surprise for you," Orion chuckles.

"You also told me that you'd talk to Uncle Colletti, remember?"

Logan tries to stifle a smile, then breaks into hearty laughter, and the rest of us join him.

Sometimes I can be a little presumptuous and pushy. But Orion did say he could help. And they haven't done anything so far.

"Patience really is a virtue, darling," Orion says.

"Fine." I pout. "Where're we heading, then?"

"We're taking you somewhere special for lunch." Orion studies me for a moment. "But I was thinking we could stop at Nubeluz for drinks first. We have some business to take care of. Would that be alright?"

"Sure." I haven't been to Nubeluz yet. It's a cool bar on the 50th floor at the Ritz-Carlton, NoMad. Lisa was talking about it last week. Apparently, it has amazing views of New York and quite a lot of cocktails on the menu.

I sit back and observe my men. Orion, Logan, and Kai are quiet, too quiet. There's something different about them. Logan strokes my hand, tracing the scar on my palm from when I had a mishap with one of his blades.

"Do you remember the first time I stitched you

up?" he asks.

I smile at the memory. "You thought you were reckless."

"I was, sweetheart." His hands cup my face and he kisses my lips softly.

Kai snickers. "I remember when you came to my match. Sat in the front row looking like sin and salvation at the same time."

"You lost that fight," I remind him.

He shrugs. "Technicalities."

The rest of the ride passes quickly, and before long, the Ritz-Carlton rises into view, glass gleaming and bathed in golden light. Emilio springs forward as we pull up, hurrying to open the door. Orion slides out first, then turns back, extending his hand to me with elegant formality. Through the opposite door, Logan and Kai slip out, nodding their thanks to the waiting valet.

I catch our reflection in the polished glass—the four of us standing shoulder to shoulder, a perfect snapshot of everything I never knew I needed. My heart swells as I gaze at them. My men. My life. Thank you, I whisper to the universe, to fate, and to Rebecca, their mother, who brought us here.

Entering the glittering rooftop bar at the Ritz is an experience. The manager appears out of nowhere and is already nodding to four servers to help us. My men are known for being ruthless. In other words, wherever they show their faces, they are feared.

The bar is full. I notice some familiar faces, but nothing's new with that. If Orion has business to do here, there will be quite a lot of our men around the place for security.

We're taken to a table that's elevated, one from where you can oversee the whole bar, and at the same time, New York. Uncle Colletti and Uncle Leo occupy the adjacent table, their acknowledgment of us brief before they return to their hushed conversation.

Crystal glasses materialize, amber whiskey gleaming in three of them.

"Maisy, what would you like to drink?" Kai asks.

I glance at their glasses, then smile at the server. "Whiskey on the rocks for me."

Orion's eyes are sweeping the bar in their usual pattern—doors, exits—but when the waiter takes my order, his gaze snaps to me. His brows arch high. "Whiskey?" The word comes out sharp, surprised. "Isn't it a bit too early for you?"

"And for you?" I retort.

"Touche, sweetheart," Logan laughs. "You can have whatever you want," he tells me.

"Of course, I'm sorry." Orion's unusual acquiescence intrigues me. Something's off.

My drink arrives instantly, ice cubes tinkling against crystal. We clink our glasses; I take a sip and look at them, my dangerous men in tailored suits with authority rolling off them in waves. They kill as easily as they breathe. But they have good hearts. And great bodies. The anticipation of their plans for me sends a delicious shiver down my spine.

The three of them face the rest of the bar, as if waiting for something.

I watch as Logan leans back in his chair, predatory grace in every movement. His gaze sweeps the bar periodically; he's always vigilant.

"So," I start, wrapping my fingers around the cool glass, "are we celebrating something?"

Orion and Logan exchange one of those looks— there's an entire conversation happening in that silence.

"You could say that, darling." Orion's voice drops lower, intimate, despite our public setting. His fingers brush against mine as he reaches for his drink, the touch deliberate.

The way he lets the sentence trail off makes heat pool between my legs. Logan's lips curve into a knowing smirk.

Uncle Colletti's deep laugh from the next table draws my attention. He's leaning forward, gesturing emphatically to Uncle Leo, who nods with the grave intensity reserved for serious family matters.

I suddenly spot Uncle Jon, along with an unusual number of our men—and women too. Even

Celina is here.

My phone buzzes, snapping me out of my thoughts. It's a text from Lisa about the women's club, but I can't focus on that right now. One question drowns out everything else: what on earth are they all doing here?

On the one hand, this is good. I can use it as leverage for my club. And I might only have minutes before they do whatever it is they came here to do. "So, how will you handle Colletti?" I ask. If they're working, I will too.

Orion locks eyes with me, his gaze intense and unwavering, transfixing me in that deep, dark way only he has. "He's a tough nut to crack," he begins, his tone measured. "But after careful consideration, we believe we've found a way to shift his perspective." He pauses, his gaze steady.

"And?" I stare at him in frustration. I hear what he's saying, but I don't understand.

He rises from the table, reaching into his pocket to retrieve a small black felt box. He lowers himself to one knee before me. Logan and Kai do the same, moving in perfect synchronization, each taking a box from their suit pocket and kneeling.

My genius brain finally catches up to what's happening.

"This is crazy," I breathe, my voice shaking.

They open the boxes simultaneously.

The bar falls into a heavy, almost eerie silence. It's so quiet, you could hear a pin drop.

Orion's eyes remain fixed on me.

"Everything we destroy, and everything we build, it's for you. Let this ring be a reminder that we will set the world ablaze to keep you safe. Will you stand with us, as a wife to be adored, and as a force to be reckoned with?"

"Marry us," they all say, almost in unison.

My throat tightens. I never thought this would be possible. "The children…"

"Are already ours," Logan reminds me. "This just makes it official."

"The families…" I'm trying to remember all the problems that are still there. This must be a mistake. They don't know it yet, but it's a mistake.

"Will be stronger when we are united," Orion finishes for me.

Tears fill my eyes, turning everything into a blurry haze. The room seems to hold its breath. It's so quiet, I can almost hear the rhythm of my own heartbeat, each thump echoing the whirlwind of emotions inside me. My ever-running thoughts flood in, louder than any external sound, as if the world itself has paused, waiting for my answer.

"Listen to your heart!" I hear someone call from

the crowd.

"Really?" My words are barely audible as I look at them, tears rolling down my cheeks. "You want me?"

They answer with actions instead of words.

Logan carefully lifts the ring from the box, his hand steady but his eyes full of emotion. Gently, he slides it onto my left ring finger, his touch warm and deliberate. As the ring settles into place, he meets my gaze and softly says, "To love you."

Orion takes his ring and carefully places it on top of Logan's, aligning it perfectly so the two fit together seamlessly. His fingers linger for a moment. Locking eyes with me, he declares, "To protect you."

Kai takes his ring and, with a steady hand, slips it onto the same finger, sliding it atop Orion's. A soft, unmistakable 'click' can be heard within the silence as the three rings lock easily into place, uniting as one. He whispers, "To fuck you."

I smile nervously, my heart pounding as I glance down at my left hand. The engagement ring, adorned with three black diamonds, glints under the light—a symbol of their unwavering claim on me, a bond as unbreakable as the stones themselves.

"Yes," I whisper. Then, louder: "Yes."

They leap to their feet with joyous exclamations, their arms wrapping around me in an embrace so full of warmth it nearly takes my breath away.

"They won't understand," I say against someone's chest.

"They don't have to," Orion says above me.

"We understand," Logan adds.

"And that's all that matters," Kai finishes.

A big cheer erupts as I wipe at my tears and look at the crowd. Everyone is here, the whole syndicate celebrating with us. Most of them must have known this was going down. Lisa waves at me from the bar and raises her glass. Celina is in her security stance, but she grins and nods at me. Angelica wipes her eyes. Georgina is here too.

I turn to see Uncle Colletti, literally staring directly at my face.

"Maisy Roy. I see there isn't a way around you."

"The world is changing, Uncle Colletti," I reply. "I hope you can see the beauty in all the women in it."

"This is a conversation for another time. Congratulations on your engagement," he says, and picks up his drink.

Kai sweeps me into his arms, spinning me in a playful circle. "You're mine now!" his laughter rolls through his chest.

I grin up at him. "Am I? I heard it's the other way around."

He sets me down gently, and Orion steps close behind me, his body warm against my back, his intent clear in the way he wraps his arms around me. "Can't wait to marry you, darling."

Logan dips down, claiming my lips in a searing kiss that steals my breath. The sudden pop of champagne corks echoes through the air like celebratory fireworks. We all turn around and see golden bubbles cascading into crystal flutes.

Cheers and whistles erupt around us, the moment crystallizing into something magical.

ONE YEAR LATER

CHAPTER 6

MAISY

The rain is relentless, a steady drumbeat against the sleek black car waiting by the curb. It's a fitting soundtrack to the months of grief and violence that have piled up like storm clouds. My heels click against the wet sidewalk, and I shiver despite the heavy coat wrapped tightly around me. I don't have to look back to know Orion, Logan, and Kai are following. Their presence is like a shadow—dark and heavy.

It wasn't a full year since our engagement when all this started happening. Instead of wedding arrangements, the only plans happening at our home are those of retaliation and revenge.

Emilio opens the car door, his face as stony as ever. He doesn't need to say anything. None of us does. The funeral already said it all—another man gone, another life stolen in this endless war we never wanted but can't seem to outrun.

I slide into the backseat; Orion follows, his movement stiff and deliberate. His bruised face is turned away, but the swollen knuckles on his bandaged hand are still evident. Logan winces as he climbs in next to me, his limp is worse today. And Kai sits opposite us, the bruising across his knuckles already darkening and his jaw muscles twitching.

The car door slams shut, and for a moment, the only sound is the rain and our collective breathing.

"They're getting bolder," Orion mutters, his voice low and hard. His silver rings catch the dim light as he rubs his good hand over his face. The bruises along his cheekbone are starting to turn purple. "Whoever's behind this isn't afraid of us anymore."

"Because we've made ourselves vulnerable," Logan says bitterly. He leans back, closing his eyes. "Three families merged into one syndicate—it was supposed to make us stronger, but there are too many moving parts, too many leaks."

"Every damn week it's another attack, another funeral." Orion lets out a sharp breath. "We don't even have time to figure out who's infiltrating us because we're too busy burying our own."

"And yet no one talks." Kai grinds his teeth. "No one saw anything. No one heard anything. We're surrounded by ghosts."

"Um…" I begin quietly, wary of the tension between them. "Not quite." It's been a while since I've had flashbacks of my past, but today, I think something came back. "I may have seen a ghost this morning at the funeral. A man in a gray suit. He had a tattoo of the sun of Vergina on his right hand. He paid his respects and left quickly, but I could swear he was one of Milan's men."

The air in the car shifts. Orion's head snaps toward me, his eyes narrowing. "You're sure?"

"As sure as I can be from a glimpse," I say, meeting his gaze.

Orion's jaw clenches and he turns to Emilio. "Drive faster."

"Drop Maisy off first," Logan adds.

I stiffen, casting my eyes between them. "Why?"

Kai sighs. "Maisy, not this again. Our life as we know it is getting too dangerous. You need to stay with the kids."

"You think I don't know it's dangerous?" My voice comes out sharper than I intended. "I've been to just as many funerals as you have. Don't tell me I can't help. My club is—"

Orion cuts me off. "We're not telling you. We're ordering you."

His words hit like a slap; I stare at him, hurt. His gaze softens for a fraction of a second, but he doesn't take it back. He never does.

They don't get it. Ever since I started the women's club, we've been quietly reshaping the syndicate, and still are. We've turned the empty warehouse into a soup kitchen where we feed hundreds of people weekly, people who then become our ears and eyes on the street. Our 'small business loans' help dozens of struggling single mothers to start legitimate enterprises, companies that could potentially help our men launder money in the future. The domestic violence rates have dropped, not just because of the self-defense classes that Celina holds on the downlow, but because word has gotten around that we protect our own. Even the corrupt cops think twice now before harassing local women—funny how quickly things change when you have leverage. We may operate in the shadows, but we are using everything we source to help our men.

Logan reaches out, his hand brushing mine. "Don't mind him," he says quietly. "He's just...We're just...We don't know what to do."

"That doesn't mean you get to shut me out," I say, my voice breaking. "I'm not just some bystander. I'm—"

"You're what keeps us grounded," Kai interrupts, his tone gentler than Orion's but just as firm. He pulls me into his side, his warmth soothing. "You're what we're trying to protect."

I lean against him, too tired to fight anymore. The adrenaline that carried me through the day is gone, leaving nothing but exhaustion and the ache of too many losses. "I just want to do something," I say. "Anything."

"You will," Logan says, "but not this."

The car falls silent again; the rain is the only sound I hear. I close my eyes, resting my head on Kai's shoulder, and try to focus on thoughts of home. Of my babies waiting for me, and Sasha and Leila looking after them. But even that comfort feels fragile, like it could shatter with the next attack.

And for some reason, something tugs at my mind. I remember our last meeting at the club, as I watched the dining room transform with each new arrival. Lisa arranged pastries on platters while Celina checked windows and doors—security habits die hard. Angelina was there; Leila too. Sasha was still flushed from chasing my children around the house, getting them ready to leave with the boys. Luckily, they didn't want her to join them that day, so she stayed for our meeting.

"Ladies," I called out, tapping at my glass with a teaspoon, "welcome to the official meeting of what

Orion, Logan, and Kai are now calling 'Rebellion Sisters.'"

Laughter rippled through the room, consisting of more than twenty powerful women ready to share secrets their husbands and boyfriends would kill to be privy to.

"He's not wrong," Lisa quipped. "Though I prefer 'Rebel Queens.' It's more dramatic."

"More accurate," Celina added, leaning against the doorway and looking sharp with her cropped hair and tailored suit.

"So." I settled into my chair at the head of the table. "Do we have any updates?"

Angelina raised her hand, gold bracelets jangling. "I finally convinced Adam to let me see the books for the shipping business."

"And?"

"They're hemorrhaging money." She rolled her eyes. "Half a million in the last quarter alone. He's been hiding it from my father."

Uncle Colletti would skin Adam alive if he knew. Better yet, I didn't even know what would happen to him when the news reached Orion. But it had been agreed that what was said here would never leave the room without prior consent.

"I could fix it in a month," Angelina continued. At thirty-two, she'd earned two business degrees before marrying Adam. Her brilliant mind was being wasted on charity galas and home decor. "Their distribution channels are prehistoric."

"Document everything," Lisa advised. "Create a solution they can't ignore."

"That's assuming they'll listen," Leila said quietly.

Our housekeeper rarely spoke at these meetings, but when she did, I listened. As one of Orion's most trusted women, she knew a lot of secrets about New York's underworld.

"Men like Uncle Colletti only hear money talking," I replied. "If Angelina can save half a million, he'll be forced to acknowledge her."

"You should just tell him," Sasha chimed in, helping herself to a pastry.

"Not a good idea. Even if your father puts you in charge." Celina turned to Angelina. "No one would want to report to a woman."

I surveyed the members of our gathering: all brilliant women, pushed to the margins of a world they understood better than the men who ruled it. Even if Orion, Logan, and Kai would listen, they still had associates or consiglieres with whom they'd have to confer. It's not easy to eradicate misogyny, that's for sure.

"This is why we need each other," Gizelle said.

"Separately, they can dismiss us. Together..." She let the implication linger.

"Together, we could run this city better than they ever could," Georgina finished. Georgina was one of the cornerstones of the club—like many of the women in that room, really.

"We basically already do," Angelina scoffed. "Who handles the legitimate business interfaces? Who maintains the social connections that keep law enforcement looking the other way? Who raises the next generation of leaders?"

"While they're playing with their guns, we're building their empires," Georgina agreed.

"You know what's funny?" Celina's voice held a dangerous edge. "If we ever decided to stage a real coup, we'd win."

The room fell silent.

"Don't look so scandalized," she continued. "We have dirt on every major player in this city, as well as further afield. We know their schedules, their weaknesses, their secret vices. Hell, we have most of them by the balls—literally."

A trickle of nervous laughter broke out.

"She's not wrong," Lisa mused. "Between us, we could probably access every important account, property deed, and blackmail file in the syndicate."

I remembered the look on Orion's face when I

first mentioned these meetings—he'd understood, even if he wouldn't admit it. We weren't just wives and sisters and daughters. We were a network, as dangerous as any rival family.

"We're not staging a coup," I clarified, though the idea sent a delicious thrill down my spine. "We're creating a partnership. The world is changing. Old ways die hard, but they do die."

"Tell that to my father," Angelina muttered.

"Actually…" I leaned forward in my seat. "I have some news. Orion, Logan, and Kai have agreed to formally present our security initiative to the council."

Celina straightened. "You're serious?"

"Dead serious. Your self-defense program will go through. They're backing us."

"Why now?" Celina asked.

"Given the threats we're facing, they worry their protection alone won't be enough," I replied. "It's not our independence that concerns them, but the risk of us becoming victims when they're not there to shield us."

As I said those words, I didn't realize just how true they were.

ORION

The wipers struggle to keep up with the rain as Emilio drives as fast as he can through the narrow streets of New York. Kai drums his swollen knuckles against the doorframe, Logan plays with his blades, and I stare out into the darkness, stuck on this fucking mess of a problem.

When we dropped Maisy home, her expression was a mix of anger and hurt as she watched us drive away. I hated leaving her like that, but I didn't have a choice. Not when we're this close to something—or someone. The man in the gray suit. Milan's man. Whoever he is, he's the key to all of this.

"This better not be a dead end," Kai mutters, breaking the silence.

"It won't be," I say, more to myself than to him. "We'll find him."

"And then what?" Logan asks as Emilio pulls up outside the funeral home.

"Logan, someone's gonna fucking die tonight, trust me," I respond, and step out into the rain as the engine stalls.

The building looms before us, the scent of damp concrete and wet asphalt lingering in the air as Kai and Logan follow me inside.

The funeral director is gone, but the security

guard barely glances up when I flash a stack of cash and a pointed glare. "We need to examine your CCTV."

The guard doesn't blink at the cash, just takes it, stands, and walks to the back like it's routine. No nod, no words, just a mechanical twist of the key in the office door.

Money talks. Always.

Inside, the room is small and cramped. The hum of the computer is the only sound as I settle into the chair. The CCTV footage is easy to pull up, and I fast-forward through hours of blurry, gray-tinted frames until I spot him. The man in the gray suit with a tattoo of a sun on his right hand. He's there, stepping into the room, his face partially obscured but that's him all right.

Kai leans over my shoulder. "Pause it."

I do, and we all study the screen in silence. He's sharp but slightly hunched, and deliberate. I press play again, and we see that he doesn't linger, doesn't make eye contact with anyone. He's in and out in under two minutes.

I switch to the footage from the outside camera.

"Get the plate," Kai says, his voice tight.

The license plate is clear enough despite the rain, and I scribble it down.

Pulling out my cell, I dial my DMV guy. After Maisy got kidnapped, the information he gave me on the vehicle from the Saudi Arabian Embassy got him into a lot of trouble. But Gerald still owes me, and I'm not in the mood to play nice. We buried a good man today.

"Orion." Gerald's voice is wary, cautious. He knows better than to take my calls lightly. "What do you need?"

"A license plate," I say brusquely. "I need the owner's details."

"I-I'm not in the office. You know I can't just—"

I cut him off. "You can, and you will. Don't make me remind you why."

There's a pause, the kind that speaks volumes. Gerald's loyalty isn't borne of respect; it's borne of fear. It's effective, if not ideal. Still, I'd like to think that he's also a buddy of mine.

"Fine," he mutters. "Give me the plate."

I rattle it off, and the line goes silent as he types. Kai paces behind me, restless and agitated and Logan stands by the door with his arms crossed.

"Got it," Gerald says finally. "Registered to a woman named Molly McKenna in Washington DC."

The words hang in the air like a gunshot. I clench the cell tighter, my mind racing. Ma Molly. The head of the Irish mafia in DC. Ruthless and unpredictable. She looked after Rosey's children when Milan was still alive. Dammit. If she's involved, this is bigger than I thought.

"Thanks," I say flatly. "You've been helpful."

"Wait, you don't want her address?" Gerard asks, but I have no time to spare.

I hang up and turn to the others. "It's Ma Molly."

Logan swears under his breath, and Kai slams his fist into the desk, making the monitor rattle. "If he's tied to Ma Molly, this could spiral fast. She's not the type to let us walk away if we make a move on her turf."

I narrow my eyes at him. "Then we make sure it doesn't spiral. This isn't about her—not yet. It's about him."

Logan holds my gaze for a moment, then nods. "Fine. But we're not going in blind."

"We never do," I snap, though the words feel hollow. Lately, it feels like we're always reacting, always one step behind. It's a position I despise.

"This doesn't make sense," Kai growls. "Why the hell would Ma Molly send someone to a funeral in New York?"

"Maybe she didn't," Logan reasons. "Maybe he's acting on his own."

I shake my head. "Not likely. Not without her knowing."

"So what's the play?" Kai's eyes dart between us. "We go to DC and ask her nicely?"

"We go to DC," I confirm, leaving no room for argument. "But not to talk to her. We're looking for him."

Logan frowns. "And if he's under her protection?"

"He can be under God's protection as far as I'm concerned, and still nothing would save him. We're just gonna make sure she doesn't know we're there."

I hate the plan, but it's the only one we've got.

Once we're back in the car, Logan's on the phone, calling in backup—one car, five of our top guys, no questions asked. These days, we don't move without extra muscle. Too many ambushes. Too many close calls.

By the time we get to the penthouse, they're already in position with the engine running.

The drive to Washington is long, the rain a constant companion as we ride. We're still in our suits; I'm sure Kai's uncomfortable by now.

By the time we reach Ma Molly's neighborhood, the rain has eased, but the air is still thick with moisture. Her house is like a fortress, sprawling and imposing, with high gates and armed guards patrolling the perimeter.

"There," Kai says, his voice low. He points to a figure lingering near the gate.

The man in the gray suit. He's talking to one of the guards, his posture hunched.

Logan squints. "Are we sure that's him?"

The man waves off the guard and crosses the street, heading toward a parked car. The tattoo on his hand clearly visible under the streetlight.

"We grab him now," I order. "Quietly."

The others nod, and we slip out of the car, moving like shadows. I gesture to those in the car behind us to be on the lookout but remain where they are, and then we wait for the guard's attention to be on the house before we pounce.

The man doesn't see us coming until it's too late.

I grab him first, my hand clamping over his mouth as Kai steps in front of him and lands a punch in his stomach.

Once he's on the ground, Logan doesn't wait; he puts duct tape over the punk's mouth as he gasps for air. "You're coming with us," he whispers.

Between the three of us, he doesn't stand a chance. We drag him to the car and I shove him into the backseat between Logan and Kai. He shoots us a glare, but it wavers—he didn't see this coming, and it shows.

Kai chuckles menacingly. "Don't worry, you'll have plenty of time to talk later."

I see the flicker of fear in his eyes as the three of us, for the first time in a while, settle back in quiet confidence. This was enough to remind us that we're not as helpless as we've been made to feel.

CHAPTER 7

LOGAN

The vault beneath my tower is damp, dark, and suffocating. The air reeks of mildew and iron, a fitting backdrop for what's about to happen. The fluorescent light flickers above us, reminding me of the one in Orion's house. It also reminds me of my own ordeal at Milan's, but I quickly shut that memory down.

Clay stands at the door, arms crossed, his muscles an immovable force that blocks any chance of escape. A Carte by blood, he's a man who's also come to be trusted by both mine and Kai's families. His eyes don't meet mine because they don't need to. Clay isn't here to question or hesitate. He's here to ensure nothing gets in—or out—that shouldn't.

Kai and I shove the man into the chair and bind his wrists to the armrests with zip ties. We pat him down, remove the duct tape from his mouth, and strip off his jacket while Orion is lining up the spoils on the steel table: a handgun, a switchblade, a small stash of cash, and—most concerningly—a compact explosive device.

"Amateur," Kai mutters as he takes off his suit jacket and loosens his tie. "Who carries a bomb like a pack of gum?"

Orion doesn't look up. He's been eerily silent, his focus entirely on the man. His bruised knuckles flex at his sides.

"Who are you?" Orion's voice cuts through the room. It's not a question; it's a command.

The man lifts his head, his lip split and swollen from the extra roughing up we gave him in the car. "I-I'm Goce. I'm nobody," he croaks. His accent is faint, but Eastern European for sure. "Y-You've got the wrong man."

Orion steps closer. "You were at the funeral," he says, his tone deep and intentional. "You knew the man we buried."

"I didn't know him." The man—Goce, if his name matters at all—glances between us. "I was paying my respects. That's all."

Kai lets out a bark of laughter. "Respect? With a

bomb in your pocket?"

The man flinches, but he doesn't answer. His silence only fuels the anger we've all been engulfed in.

Orion grabs a pair of pliers from the table, but he's not rushing; he's savoring the moment, letting the man's fear build.

"You're gonna tell us the truth," he says, his voice cold as death, "or I'll start removing pieces of you until you do."

"You're insane," Goce spits, but the tremor in his voice betrays him.

Orion grips the man's jaw, forcing it open. "Hold still now," he murmurs, almost gently, before clamping the pliers around a tooth. The scream that follows echoes throughout the vault.

Goce breaks faster than I expect. After the second tooth, he's squealing, words tumbling from his mouth like a dam has burst. "Alright! Alright! I'll talk!"

Orion steps back, tossing the bloodied pliers onto the table. "We're waiting."

Goce gulps for air, his chest heaving. "There's...There's a new boss in town," he says, his words frantic. "He came about a year ago. From Ireland. But he's not Irish. Ma Molly's his aunt. Was," he finishes, and spits blood all over himself.

"Was?" I can't hide my surprise. "She's dead?"

"It was him," Goce says. "She welcomed him.

Called him a nephew. Told everyone he was family. And then he killed her. Made it look like an accident."

Logan's fists tighten. "And now he's taken over DC? Just like that?"

Goce nods, his eyes darting around the room. "He's ruthless. He's...a Slav. From North Macedonia. That's all I know."

The S-word hangs in the air, heavy with implications. I exchange a glance with Orion, and I can see the same thought reflected in his eyes.

"What does he want?" Orion's voice is deceptively calm.

"New York," Goce whispers. "He knows the city used to be split four ways. The Slavs...they were part of that. He wants his share. His twenty-five percent."

"And the attacks?" Kai presses. "All the dead men? That's him?"

Goce hesitates, then nods. "He's testing you. Weakening you. He knows about the three families. He knows you're spread thin. And he knows Maisy—"

The mention of her name sends a ripple of tension through the room. Orion steps forward, his shadow engulfing the man in the chair. "What about Maisy?"

"N-Nothing," Goce stammers. "I don't know. Just rumors. That's all. Please. I've told you everything."

Kai's hand shoots out, clamping around Goce's

throat. "What rumors?"

The man's eyes widen and he starts to choke, sputtering as his face reddens.

"Kai," Orion says sharply. "We don't wanna kill him. Not yet."

Fuck, when will he learn to keep his emotions in check?

For a moment, it feels like Kai will kill him right here, in front of our eyes. The room is heavy with his anger, but finally, his grip loosens. Goce collapses forward, coughing and gasping for air.

"What. Rumors?" Kai growls through clenched teeth.

Goce's hands shake as he clutches the arms of the chair, his breath ragged. "W-With her out of the way, he can...he can be part of the syndicate, and rule. As a Slav," he rasps, his words spilling out like a confession.

The moment Goce's done, Kai's fist connects with his jaw with a brutal, unrestrained swing. The sound of bone meeting flesh echoes around the room, and Goce's head snaps back before he slumps, unconscious, within his restraints.

The room falls into a deafening silence, broken only by the faint buzz of the overhead light. Orion doesn't move at first, his expression unreadable as his gaze shifts between Kai and the unconscious man. Then he steps in, grips the man's head—one hand at the base, the other clamped around his jaw—and twists with brutal precision. There's a sharp snap, sudden and final, as the body goes limp in his arms.

He turns to Clay. "We don't need him any longer. Take him away."

Clay nods without a word, his massive frame slouching over Goce while he cuts his restraints before hoisting him over his shoulder as if he weighs nothing. The sound of heavy footsteps echoes down the stone corridor as Clay disappears with the limp body, leaving the rest of us in the oppressive quiet.

Kai stands rigid, his fists still clenched, his knuckles white. I exhale slowly, the weight of Goce's words pressing down on me. Her name lingers in the air like a curse, and I can't shake the feeling that this is only the beginning of something far worse than any of us are prepared for.

Kai breaks the silence first. "A Slav boss. In DC. And he's coming to New York. For Maisy."

I nod slowly. "This changes everything."

Orion's gaze hardens. "No. The stakes are just higher. But we've dealt with worse."

MAISY

The sound of Ava's soft giggle fills the nursery, followed by Grace's high-pitched hum of contentment. Their tiny faces glow in the soft light from the elephant-shaped nightlight, the only source of illumination in the room. I tuck the blanket tighter around Ava as she nestles into Orion's shoulder, her eyes fluttering closed. Beside her bed, Grace's hands clutch at her favorite stuffed fox as I lean over to kiss her forehead.

"Night, night, sweetheart," I whisper, smoothing down her dark curls.

Orion murmurs something low to Ava, something I can't quite catch, but it makes her giggle again before sleep finally claims her. His deep voice is so different here, softer, more tender, almost as if he's afraid to break the spell of this quiet moment. It tugs at something deep in my chest—a combination of warmth and unease. Orion has always been good at making me feel both.

I was waiting on them to tell me where they'd disappeared to, and what they'd done. But I got nothing. Instead, they simply changed clothes and slipped seamlessly into our evening ritual, as though they hadn't vanished for hours without explanation.

Now, they move through the familiar choreography of bedtime. I pull back to stand beside

Orion as he gently settles Ava into her bed. Orion in his black sweatpants and t-shirt is a sight I've come to cherish. It totally mollifies me.

He pauses, looking down at the twins before whispering, "Sweet dreams, girls."

We step into the hallway and close the nursery door as quietly as possible. Across from us, I hear enthusiastic chatter coming from Maxim's room. I can picture Logan perched on the edge of his bed, probably trying to answer the endless stream of questions Maxim always seems to have at bedtime.

"Why doesn't the moon stay full all the time, Dad?" Maxim asks, loudly enough for his words to carry into the hall.

Logan's calm voice follows, warm with patience. "Because the Earth gets in the way sometimes. It's called phases. I'll show you how it works tomorrow, alright? But now, it's time to sleep."

Maxim doesn't seem convinced, but after a little more reassurance and a quick hug, Logan emerges from his room, brushing a hand through his hair. His eyes meet mine, and he offers a tired smile before heading into Luca's room next door, who's usually the first to fall asleep, never bothered by the noise from any of his siblings.

In the room to the left, Damien's laughter rings out like bells, high-pitched and unrestrained. I peek inside and find Kai tossing him onto the bed like a ragdoll, earning delighted shrieks from him as well as Mila, who is half-laughing, half-protesting. "You're doing it all wrong!" Mila declares, her little hands perched on her hips.

Kai grins, unrepentant. "Oh? And how should it be done, Miss Expert?"

Mila rolls her eyes but moves forward with surprising authority for a four-year-old. "Like this," she says, buttoning up Damien's pajama top with quick, precise movements. Kai watches with exaggerated admiration, nodding at her every move like she's conducting the world's most important lesson. By the time Mila climbs into bed, her expression is smug, and Kai plants a kiss on the top of her head before whispering something that makes her giggle again.

Eventually, the four of us gather by the nursery door to exchange a few quiet words. I take one last glance into the bedrooms before flipping the hallway lights off. The kids are asleep already, their little bodies worn out from the day.

We head downstairs and enter the living room, but the peace that settles over the house feels strained. Logan and Kai flop down on the couch and Orion sits in his leather armchair. There's a heaviness in the air that has nothing to do with exhaustion. I can feel it radiating from the three men, each of them holding something back. I know them too well to ignore it.

"You're all too quiet," I say, looking between them. "What did you find out?"

"Let's not talk about it tonight." Orion's tone of voice leaves no room for argument.

I raise an eyebrow but let it go, at least for now. Instead, I force a smile, trying to lighten the mood. "Fine. Let's watch a movie, then."

Kai narrows his eyes at me, suspicion creeping into his expression. "Since when do you let us off the hook that easy?"

"Since I decided you all look like you could use a break," I reply, already heading for the home theatre. "Now, no excuses."

The home theatre is one of my favorite places in the house. It's cozy despite its size, with oversized cushions scattered across the floor and recliners lining the back wall.

With little objection, the three of them follow me inside. It's like they're trying too hard not to argue with me. Which really is a sign that there is, in fact, something going on.

"I'll make popcorn," I announce, and head out to the kitchen. "Orion, come help me."

Orion follows, together with his dark mood, the one that clearly makes him want to avoid difficult discussion. In the kitchen, I start gathering supplies, aware of his presence behind me. He fumbles with the popcorn machine and says nothing at first, but I can feel his gaze on me, steady and intent.

"You're terrible at this," I say eventually, shooting him a teasing look. "How does a man who controls everything else in his life fail so miserably at making popcorn?"

His lips quirk into a smirk, his voice dropping into that low, dangerous tone that always makes my pulse jump. "Maybe I'm not trying to make popcorn at all."

Heat rushes to my cheeks as he steps closer.

"Maybe..." he mumbles against my lips, reaching down with one hand to lift the edge of my dress. The soft fabric glides up my thigh and he pulls gently, raising it higher. "Maybe I'm trying to find out if you're wet..." With his other hand, he pushes my hair back over my shoulder and nuzzles at my neck. "...so I can fuck you, my little slut." He pulls my panties to one side and unhurriedly runs two fingers along my hot, wet entrance a few times. My arousal surges at his touch.

"Orion," I sense my heat dripping onto his fingers as pleasure burns through me.

"Just what I thought," he growls as he inserts his fingers deep inside me, making me moan as I feel him everywhere in my body. But it's over too soon, and he pulls his fingers away.

"More?" he snickers, and skillfully slides my panties down, kneeling as he does, his gaze fixed on me. I watch his every move, the fire in his dark eyes searing into mine.

He takes me with him as he straightens up, lifting me onto the kitchen counter. Then, as he plants the most potent kiss on my mouth, deep enough for me to feel the sudden rush of wet heat in my core, his hands land on my inner thighs and he forces my legs open. He ends our kiss and gets me to plant my hands behind me for support, and just like that, I've given him access to all of me. He lowers his head, inhales deeply, and growls his approval as he presses the flat of his tongue against my opening. His touch sends a shiver up the length of my spine and I whimper shamelessly as he works the tip inside me, then licks the length of my cunt.

"Orion," I pant as he swirls his tongue over my clit, the rush of my arousal between my thighs making me open up to him even more.

"This should be illegal, it's so good," he hisses against me as he sucks my clit into his mouth and pushes two fingers inside me at the same time. My back arches in pleasure. I'm trying to raise my hips, to grind myself against his mouth. I sense my climax coming, a massive wave, ready to tear through me and leave my whole body trembling.

I rake my fingers through his hair and pull his

head closer, if that is at all possible, as he tips me over the edge.

"Orion!" My legs tremble violently as I ride the wave he serves me, while his tongue and his fingers work me into a frenzy. I'm losing any control I have, flying like this, with him. I'm being undone, piece by piece.

I'm panting and have barely come down from my high when he comes up, wraps one arm around my waist, and pulls me to him. With the other hand, he pulls down his sweatpants and frees his hard cock, the piercing glistening with precum.

"I'm not done with you yet." He runs his cock up and down my slit, and when he's satisfied that I can take him, he lifts me by the butt cheeks and spears my body, entering me to his balls, fully stretching my pussy. "Oh, fuck yes!" he growls.

I moan and wrap my arms around his shoulders, pulling his body closer to me with sweet urgency as he groans into my neck.

Holding onto my body for leverage, he begins to pound into me, hard and fast, wordless grunts falling from his throat.

I'm slammed into him as his arms wrap tight around me; I can barely breathe. Each thrust into my pussy is ruthless. I whimper, taken to a different kind of high, a different climax that I welcome, and when I hear his grunts become staccato, I fully unravel, writhing and crying out.

"Orion...Orion!" I lower my head to his shoulder and release a loud moan, almost simultaneously with his long groan as he empties his balls into me.

It takes me a while to come back down from the heights I've visited. I'm still out of breath, panting, when I hear his sigh.

"Fuck, I needed this." He presses his lips to mine before sliding his cock out.

"I know," I say as he lowers me down from the counter.

He finds my panties and helps me put them on while his cum trickles down my inner thighs. "Don't wash up. You got more men to fuck tonight."

Fresh heat rushes between my legs and I'm turned on again, as if my pussy is operated by a tap. I laugh and press my lips to his, humming against his mouth.

I turn to the popcorn machine and pour the kernels inside. Before I can step back, Orion's arms slide around my waist, and he tucks his face into the curve of my neck. His warmth seeps into me as we stand there, listening to the soft pops that fill the silence.

Tonight, I'll play nice. But after this? I'm done pretending. I'll dig for answers until they break.

Once we're done, as if nothing has happened, but certainly flushed, I return to the room with a large bowl of popcorn and lie down on the cushions right between Logan and Kai. Orion hovers by the door.

"Why don't you three play tonight? I'm heading to bed," Orion states matter-of-factly. He's had his fill, just what he wanted, and he's ready to sleep now.

"I was gonna suggest the same thing after hearing you 'make popcorn' a moment ago." Kai makes air quotes with his fingers, and I cannot help but giggle.

Orion flips him the bird.

Logan is browsing through the movies and sniggering. "Let him be, Kai. He's got so much on his plate that he's even started to eat from the kitchen counter. Right, Orion?"

The three of us burst into laughter as Orion flips his other middle finger and stifles a grin before leaving the room.

"I like playful Orion," I say, still giggling.

"You do that to him, Maisy," Logan reminds me. "To us."

~

I was looking forward to playing with both Kai and Logan, but that never happened. As we were getting into it, I started making inquiries, asking a few innocent questions. I thought I might get the answers they've so far failed to give me and then we'd have sex. That usually works. There were only a few things that I wanted to know. But they saw through me, and that was it. All of a sudden, they didn't feel like having sex. They didn't want sex. They were tired. Kai and Logan.

They were evading something.

Needless to say, we didn't even start let alone finish a movie, and we went to bed instead.

Right now, I really want to know, and I'm more awake than ever. I turn to Orion, my voice cutting through the silence in the room. "Orion, what did you learn from Milan's man?"

Orion sighs. He must have sensed something might be off due to us coming to bed in silence only minutes after him. It takes him a minute before he responds. "That this war isn't over. It's only just begun."

My heart sinks. "What does that mean?"

"It means we fight," Kai responds. "But we agree on one thing. You're staying out of it."

The words hit like a slap. I sit up and face the three of them. With the moonlight spilling through the window, I see their faces, their troubled expressions. "What aren't you telling me?"

There's a long pause before I hear Orion's voice. "There's a new asshole on the scene. And he's after New York."

"Who is he?"

"We don't know. Someone from North

Macedonia," Logan mutters. "A Slav."

"A Slav?" I frown. Now I understand the reason behind their behavior.

"And to claim New York, he has to take you out," Kai finishes.

A cold wave of fear rolls over me. "Take me out? Why me?"

"Why do you think?" Orion hisses.

That's just not fair. "It's not my fault I'm a Slav, Orion! I'll stand and fight!"

"No," Kai says sharply. "We're not letting that happen."

"You're going to Chicago with the kids. You'll be safe there," Orion says with finality.

"Safe? Do you think running makes me safe? Makes us safe?"

"Maisy," Logan says gently, "this isn't about running. It's about protecting you—and our family."

"Why Chicago? Who's there?"

"I have a trusted contact in Chicago," Logan says gently, as if to make me feel better. "They'll look after you, Maisy. And our children. You'll see."

"You trust them enough that you'd send your children there? Miles away from home?"

"Yes, I do," he states firmly.

My eyes have adjusted to the darkness, and I can see their faces clearly. I falter for a moment, the mention of the kids tugging at my resolve. But then I square my shoulders, meeting their gazes head-on. "I won't go."

"You don't get a say in it." Orion's tone never leaves room for argument. He turns his back to me. "Now sleep."

CHAPTER 8

MAISY

I stir in bed to the faint sounds of hurried whispers and footsteps coming from down the hall. Something's wrong. I know it before I'm even fully awake.

The door creaks open, and there they are. Orion steps in first, tall, too somber for my liking, fully dressed in his impeccable three-piece suit. But that's nothing new, as he's always up early. Behind him, Logan's also dressed up in a three-piece suit. Now I know something's up. Logan would usually be in his white coat, ready for a shift at the hospital. I glance at Kai behind them and he, too, is not his usual self, wearing dark jeans and a black t-shirt. This means he's staying in and working. Which is not that common for him.

Suddenly, my heart's racing.

"Get up," Orion orders.

"What's going on?"

Logan steps forward, his tone gentler but no less resolute. "The kids are packed, Maisy. You need to get ready. We're taking you to the airport."

The words hit like a punch in the stomach. I blink at them, my mind scrambling to process their words. "Airport? What are you talking about?"

"You're going to Chicago," Kai says, his voice clipped. "You'll all be safe there."

Safe. There's that word again. It ignites something sharp and furious in my chest. "No," I say, swinging my legs over the side of the bed and standing up. "Absolutely not."

Orion's jaw tightens. "This isn't up for discussion."

"You don't get to make that decision for me." I ball my hands into fists but don't raise them. Never at them.

"Actually, we do," Kai cuts in. "We're not gonna just sit here and let him come for you, or the kids. You're leaving, Maisy. End of story."

Hot and unrelenting anger surges through me. "I'm not some pawn you can move around on a board! If he's coming, I'm staying. I'll fight."

"You're a mother now," Logan reminds me, like I don't already know. "Your job is to protect our kids, not play the hero."

"And your job," I shoot back, pointing a finger at him, "is to let me decide how I protect them."

Orion steps closer. "We're not doing this. Get dressed. Pack light. We're leaving in thirty minutes."

"Noo!" The word tears from me like a battle cry. I shove past them, but Kai's hand shoots out, grabbing my wrist.

"Don't make this harder than it needs to be." He grips me tight as I glare at him.

I yank my arm free. "You think this is hard? Try being the one who has to run while the people she loves fight her battles."

Kai looks away, his jaw clenched, and for a moment, I think I've gotten through to him. But then Orion steps between us, his gaze cutting into mine like a blade.

"We don't have time for this," he says. "Go get ready."

The finality in his tone leaves no room for argument. I turn on my heel and storm toward the bathroom, slamming the door behind me. My chest heaves with anger, frustration, and something deeper— something that feels a lot like fear. Like when I was running. Like...like the beginning. Uncertainty.

I press my palms against the cool marble of the sink, staring at my reflection. I can't do this. I can't just leave.

Grabbing my cell from the counter, I dial Angelina's number. She answers on the second ring.

"Maisy?" Her voice is groggy, confused. I haven't checked the time; it must be early for her. "What's going on?"

"I need a huge favor," I say quickly, my voice low. "I need you to get Celina and meet me at JFK in a half hour."

"Why? What happened?"

"Listen to me very carefully, Angelina. I trust you with the lives of all my children, so you and Celina better come through for me. You hear me?"

"W-Where are we taking them?"

"Tell your husband you're going on a girls' vacation with Celina. And say nothing else."

"Maisy, that's—"

She hesitates, but I cut her off. I don't have time for explanations. "Can you do it?"

"Yes," she says. "We'll be there. Are you okay?"

"No," I admit, my voice trembling, "but I will be. I just...I need my children as far away from here as possible."

I won't let my children be part of any mafia war, let alone mine.

I hang up and set the cell down, my hands shaking. For a moment, I just stand there, the reality of the situation crashing down around me. They're trying to protect me, I know that. But they're wrong. Running won't solve anything. Whoever wants to take me out, they'll have to face me first.

A knock jolts me from my thoughts.

"Maisy." Logan's voice comes from the other side of the door. "We need to leave."

I take a deep breath, steadying myself. "Give me a minute."

"We don't have a minute," comes Orion's voice, sharper this time.

I open the door, chin raised in defiance. They're all standing there, their expressions a mix of frustration and pain. Without a word, I cross to my closet and extract a knee-length black dress. I slip it on without bothering to change my underwear. Apparently, there's no time for a shower.

"How long should I pack for?" I ask as I carefully start adding clothes to the open suitcase that's been placed on the bed. I need to know exactly how long I'm supposed to be away.

They go quiet for a moment. Then, from somewhere behind me, I hear Orion. "At least a month."

I turn to object, ready to yell at him, but he gestures coldly at me by raising his hand. "That's enough clothes. Let's go."

Outside the house, Emilio stands beside the family car. The trunk is open and I see the double stroller, together with the kids' luggage, already packed and stacked neatly. Sasha is here too, holding Ava in one arm and wrangling with Damien with the other. Her calm efficiency should reassure me, but it doesn't. All this just looks sad.

I'm not ready to leave. They are pushing me out.

Orion, Logan, and Kai stand near the door; I'm certain they hate all of this, but they have this visceral need to protect me and the kids, no matter what. I can't go against them. They've made up their minds, and nothing I say or do will change that.

Once again, I state my feelings loud and clear. "I don't want to go."

"Maisy," Logan says softly, "this is what's best for you and for our kids."

"And what about you?" I raise my voice. "What happens to you while I'm gone?"

"Don't worry about us, baby girl. We've got this," Kai says, steady and sure, but it doesn't ease the weight in my chest. I know what's at stake if things go south.

"What if you all die? Then what? I'll be all alone, just like when I came into this world." My eyes flood with tears. "I don't want to go," I repeat.

I look to Orion, the one who always seems to have the answer, who always knows what to say to keep me grounded. But he just stares straight ahead with no emotion. "You're getting in that car. Whether you want to or not."

The tears sting; I can't stop them. I blink rapidly, unwilling to let them fall, but it's useless. My throat burns, my chest aches, and the fight in me that's always been so instinctive feels like it's slipping through my fingers.

"Why?" My voice cracks. "Why do you get to decide? Why do you think you can protect me better by sending me away?"

"Because we know what's coming," Orion says, his gaze meeting mine with a hardness that makes me flinch. "And if you're here, Maisy, you're gonna be in the middle of it."

From inside the house, I hear the rest of the children's laughter getting louder, and before I can respond, they're all outside. Mila is holding Grace's hand, their matching curls bouncing as they run. Maxim trails behind, dragging a small backpack, while Luca chatters excitedly to Leila about some imaginary adventure they're about to go on.

"Mommy, why are you crying?" Mila's eyes are wide with concern as she reaches for my hand.

I crouch down, quickly brushing away the tears

as I force a smile. "I'm just...going to miss you all so much."

"But we're going together!" Damien pipes up, his little face lighting up as he grabs Mila's other hand. "We're going on an adventure, right, Mommy?"

"Right," I whisper, though the word feels like a betrayal. "An adventure."

The kids are ushered around by Sasha, who gives me a small, knowing smile as she passes me. She doesn't say anything—she doesn't need to. She's been with us long enough to understand what this is, even if the kids don't.

Emilio steps forward, opening the car door and making my stomach churn. He's acting as if today is just like any other day. The kids climb in one by one, their giggles and chatter a stark contrast to the heaviness in my heart. Each of them has their own seat in the family car, with safety protocols in place. When it's my turn to climb in, I hesitate, gripping the doorframe as though it might anchor me to the ground.

Orion steps closer. "Maisy, don't make this harder than it already is."

I turn to him, the tears spilling over now. "It doesn't have to be this way."

"It does," Logan says. "Maisy, please. Just go. For them."

The lump in my throat makes it hard to speak. I

glance back at the kids, and at Sasha, who's already buckling Grace into her seat. They're my everything. My reason for fighting, and for surviving. And no matter how much it tears me apart, no matter how much I want to scream and fight and run back into the house, right now, I can't do anything.

I climb into the car, my hands trembling as I settle into my seat. Emilio closes the door behind me with a stoic expression on his face. I glance out the window, my gaze locking onto Orion, Logan, and Kai. They're standing together, their faces drawn and somber.

"Mommy, are you okay?" Maxim asks, his small hand reaching for mine.

I nod, forcing another smile as I squeeze his hand tightly. "I'm okay, sweetheart. Just tired."

He seems satisfied with the answer, leaning his head against my arm as he chats with Luca about what movies they'll watch on the plane.

As the car pulls away and turns the corner, the house disappears, and with it, the three men who've become my entire world. My chest tightens and I bite back a sob, closing my eyes to keep the tears from falling again.

We speed down the highway, Emilio carrying me further away from everything I know, from everything I've fought so hard to protect. The kids' chatter from the backseat fills the car, but Sasha is the one who keeps them entertained, handing out snacks and fielding their endless questions about planes and adventures. I should be grateful for her, but all I can focus on is the crushing knot in my chest.

I shift in my seat and automatically check out the surrounding vehicles, and notice two black cars following closely behind us. I catch Emilio's eyes in the rearview mirror.

"Emilio," I say, "do you know there are two cars following us?"

He glances at the side mirror, his hands tightening slightly on the steering wheel. "They're our men," he says simply. "To watch over you. Just in case."

I wipe my cheeks. "Just in case of what? You think someone's going to ambush us on the way to the airport?"

"It's a precaution," he replies. "Orion's orders."

Of course, it's Orion. I sink back into my seat. Typical. Even when he's not physically here, he's pulling the strings, making decisions for me without so much as asking what I want. I glance out the rear window at the two sleek black cars trailing us at a careful distance. It feels like overkill, but then again, everything about this situation feels like overkill.

"We're almost there," Emilio says as the airport signs flash past.

The car slows as we pull into the busy drop-off

area outside JFK airport. Crowds of travelers move in every direction, dragging luggage, clutching tickets, their voices blending into a cacophony that almost overwhelms me.

Emilio parks the car and steps out, coming around to open my door. I hesitate, gripping the door handle. My body feels frozen, like my mind and heart are at war. I don't want to get out. I don't want to step into that airport, to do something I may regret. I changed my mind too many times on the way here. I'm looking back at the kids—at Mila's wide eyes, at Ava clutching her stuffed fox—and I don't know if I have a choice.

"Mommy, why are we here?" Maxim asks, his little face scrunched in confusion.

"We're going on a trip, sweetheart," I manage, my voice trembling. I step out of the car, my legs unsteady beneath me. Emilio offers a hand but I wave him off. I can do this. I have to do this.

Sasha's already unloaded the luggage and is expertly opening the double stroller. She glances at me, her expression softening. "It'll be okay," she says kindly.

I nod, though I don't believe her. My hands tremble as I buckle Ava and Grace into the stroller.

Behind me, I catch a glimpse of Martin, one of the men from the trailing cars. I know who he is before I even see the earpiece or the slight tilt of his head as he murmurs into his cell. Orion's right-hand man. Tall, broad-shouldered, with a stoic expression that reminds me too much of Orion. He lingers at a distance, his eyes scanning the crowd.

I can practically hear Orion's voice on the other end of the line, asking for updates, demanding to know if I've boarded my plane yet.

Sasha takes charge of the older kids and starts ushering them toward the entrance while I hang back. My heart's pounding. Emilio watches me, waiting for me to say something, to fight back. But I don't. I can't. Not with the kids so close, not with Martin and the others watching my every move.

I force myself to follow Sasha, pushing the stroller, my steps slow and heavy. The crowd presses in around us, a sea of strangers with no idea that my world is crumbling. As we approach the security checkpoint, I glance back one last time. Martin stands by a pillar, his cell pressed to his ear, his sharp gaze fixed on me. He nods once, a subtle acknowledgment that feels like a goodbye.

"Maisy, we need to keep moving," Sasha says gently, her hand on my arm.

I nod, swallowing the lump in my throat as we step through the security and metal detectors. The kids are still chattering, oblivious to the chaos consuming me from the inside.

As we head toward our departure gate, I can't

help but glance over my shoulder again. Martin's gone. Probably on his way to report back to Orion.

The thought of him sends a fresh wave of anger through me. I know they're doing this because they love me. Because they're terrified of losing me. But I hate being forced into running, and all I want is to scream and fight and turn back.

"Mommy, are you okay?" Mila asks, tugging on my sleeve.

I crouch down, brushing her hair back and forcing another smile. "I'm okay, sweetheart. I promise."

She looks at me for a long moment, then glances behind me, her big eyes widening in surprise. "Auntie Angelina! Auntie Celina!"

I turn. Angelina and Celina are both carrying small bags, grinning from ear to ear, their arms spread open. I suppose they do look like they are ready to spend time with six little devils.

Angelina hugs Mila. "Hi, sweetheart!"

Celina turns to the rest of the children. "Hey guys, I hear we're going on an adventure!" she says warmly.

"Are you coming with us?" Damien asks, bouncing on his toes, his energy impossible to contain.

"Can we go to the beach? I want to build the biggest sandcastle ever!" Luca chimes in, his imagination already getting ahead of him.

Damien wraps himself around Celina's leg. "You are coming, aren't you?"

They all exclaim excitedly as she kneels to their level, her eyes twinkling with affection. "Of course we are! We're gonna have so much fun!"

Before they take over, I motion for Sasha to take the children away. She manages to unglue Mila from Angelina and huddles the kids close; she's great at distracting them. I can already see her words lighting up their little faces with excitement.

Celina stands back up and looks at me. Her brow furrows and she crosses her arms. "Maisy, what the hell is going on?" she hisses.

I take a slow breath, forcing the tension from my shoulders. "I need a favor."

Angelina's gaze sharpens. "What kind of favor involves six kids and an unplanned flight out of New York?"

I exhale, glancing at the children before meeting my friends' eyes. "The syndicate's been hit too many times. You know that. We see each other more at funerals than at parties these days. Orion, Logan, and Kai want the kids out of New York."

"And you?" Angelina asks, as if she doesn't know what I'm going to say.

I shake my head. "I'm gonna stay."

Celina's jaw tightens. "Then I'm staying too."

"No," I cut in, firm. "I need you with them. I trust only you and Angelina for this task."

Angelina hesitates, glancing at Celina before looking back at me. "You know this is insane, right?"

I nod. "Probably."

Celina's lips press into a thin line. "Where are we flying to?"

"Chicago," I explain, gesturing to Sasha. "She'll be coming with you, too. There'll be a cab waiting there to take you somewhere safe."

Angelina shakes her head. "What are you going to do, Maisy?"

I swallow the lump in my throat. "Whatever I have to."

She studies me for a moment. "And you want us to just take them and pretend this is fine?"

"No," I say quietly. "I want you to help me. And I'll meet you there in a week. Tops."

Angelina exhales, twisting the ring on her finger.

"What did you tell your husband?" I ask her.

"Nothing yet." She sighs. "But I'm gonna have to tell him I'm in Chicago."

"Sure. But no one else." I must keep all this under control.

"Don't worry, no one will find out," Celina promises.

My children, oblivious to the tension, chatter

amongst themselves. Grace and Ava are dozing off in the stroller. I kneel, pulling them close, pressing kisses into their hair and inhaling the scent of them, willing myself to be strong.

"You'll go with your aunties and Sasha, and I'll get to you as soon as I can," I say, kissing their foreheads. "You'll have so much fun, and when I come, you'll tell me all about it, okay?"

Maxim grins. "Can we go to Disneyland?"

Angelina laughs softly, ruffling his hair. "Absolutely. We'll take you to Disneyland, eat too much cotton candy, and make sure you have the best time."

Their excitement makes my chest constrict, the sharp sting of guilt settling deep. I should be going with them. I should be making them safe myself.

I squeeze their hands, kiss their heads one last time, and stand. "Go," I tell Angelina and Celina. "And keep them safe."

Angelina nods, giving me one final, meaningful look before guiding the children toward security. I stand there and wave, exchanging nods with Sasha as well. As I watch them disappear into the crowd, I feel something inside me splinter.

I put on a cap that I shoved into my purse as I was leaving, and turn on my heel, slipping out through the airport unnoticed. My hand reaches for my cell, and I dial Georgina's number. "I need a place to stay.

Somewhere no one will find me."

She gives me an address without asking any questions, and I quickly make a note of it before I switch it off and hail a cab.

CHAPTER 9

ORION

I watch the car disappear around the corner, taking Maisy and our children away from danger. The painful feeling in my chest expands with each second they're gone. I turn to Logan and Kai, their expressions mirroring how I feel.

"Penthouse," I say simply. They nod, no words needed between us.

We take my car there. As I drive, my hands grip the steering wheel so tight my knuckles are white, and I can hear the blood pounding in my ears. The only thing louder is the sound of my own rage, crackling under my skin.

This is the only thing we were afraid of. The only

thing.

"For fuck's sake!" I growl, slamming my palm against the steering wheel hard enough to make the horn blare. "We should've married her a year ago!"

"We should have," Logan mutters beside me, jaw clenched, "but we had to explain to her what it would mean. And that was a conversation no one was ready to have with her."

"We were cowards," I spit out. "Might as well have tied a ribbon around her and paraded her among every scumbag who wants a piece of New York."

Kai leans forward from the back seat. "She doesn't give a damn about New York, honestly. She's not in this for the politics."

I let out a bitter laugh. "Have you seen her lately? Running that club like it's her own little empire?" I shoot a glance at Logan, who doesn't bother to answer. He doesn't have to. We all know it's true. Maisy might not care about politics, but she knows power. And she's no fool.

"That's exactly why she should've been ours already," I say, my voice rising. "Why the fuck did we wait, huh? Tell me, why?!"

I slam the steering wheel again, the sharp crack echoes inside the vehicle. My other hand comes off the wheel as I gesture wildly, adrenaline buzzing. "All these murders—every single one of them—could've been avoided! No one would've dared challenge us if she were legally ours. It would've been family business. By every law, by every fucking code that exists in this world. And she would've been safe. Safe!"

Kai speaks sharply. "She is safe."

"Yeah, but for how long, Kai?" I bark. "From day one, she's been a target."

"True, the problem could've been fixed by marrying her," Logan says firmly, trying to make sense of it for all of us. "But it's too late now."

And that's the damn truth.

It's too late now.

I pull into the underground parking of the penthouse building and shut off the engine. We sit there for a moment, none of us moving.

Kai opens his door first. Logan follows. I don't.

I stare at the steering wheel, rage simmering under my skin. But underneath that? Guilt. A deep, ugly guilt that digs its claws into my ribs and won't let go.

She trusted us.

Maisy, with her naïve intelligence and reckless laugh. With that fierce heart of hers that somehow cracked all three of us open without her even trying.

She trusted us, and we waited.

We waited until the enemy moved first.

I finally get out of the car and follow the others to the elevator.

In my head, I'm already running plans and scenarios for defeating this asshole. He's crossed a line that cannot be uncrossed. By simply involving Maisy in this, he's signed his death warrant—he just doesn't know it yet.

When we arrive, Uncle Colletti and Uncle Leo are waiting, ready to lay out the insider information they've uncovered.

"His name's Viktor Mrozovski," Uncle Coletti says. "He's here to claim New York. His three brothers are to join him soon. If they haven't already."

My jaw tightens as I listen to him. Kai tenses beside me, his arms crossed over his chest. Logan remains motionless. There's no reaction, no sharp intake of breath, but I know them both too well. We're all mapping out the different ways we could kill this motherfucker.

"Maisy's the only one who can challenge his claim, so he probably wants her dead." Coletti exhales, waiting for us to take in this last piece of information.

The silence that follows could be cut with a knife.

"And—they're Slavs," Coletti concludes.

"Maisy's the reason for all of this," Uncle Leo sneers, his tone dripping with arrogance. In any other situation, he'd already be dead, but that smug bastard knows I'm powerless. He knows I need him—hell, I need all of them—and he's using it against me.

The muscle in my jaw ticks and I look away. I should have seen this coming. The moment we unified the families, we became vulnerable. Too many people to control, too many cracks in our security. And now, because of her name, because of who she is, because of her stake in New York, we're in the middle of a war.

I don't regret Maisy. I don't regret the life we've built with her, or our beautiful children. But I do regret how exposed it's left us. How exposed it's left her.

The buzzing of my cell shatters the silence. I grab it to see Emilio's name flashing up on the screen. I answer instantly. "Talk to me."

His voice is ragged, panicked. "Someone's shooting at me!"

My blood turns to ice. "Where are you?"

"On the highway," he snaps. "I can't see the car!"

"Emilio's taking fire," I tell everybody in the room. Logan shoots to his feet. Kai mutters a curse under his breath. Uncle Coletti and Uncle Leo are watching me intently.

"Can you shake them?" I ask.

"I'm trying."

"Then do it. Stay low," I order. "And don't come out until I say. Got it?"

"Got it."

The line clicks dead, and I slam my cell onto the

desk. "They know we pulled Maisy out of New York."

Kai's voice tightens. "What's stopping them from going after her?"

Logan doesn't hesitate; he's already pulling out his cell. "I'll call my Chicago contact!"

"She's gonna bring trouble with her," I say, more to myself than to them. "They won't stop."

Uncle Leo shifts in his chair, rubbing his jaw. "So, what's the plan, boys?" he asks, his tone dry. "You gonna sit here and wait for him to come knocking? Or are you gonna take care of it first?"

Kai exhales harshly and looks at me. "We don't wait."

Logan nods. "We hit first."

I roll my shoulders, forcing the tension in my muscles to ease. There's no other option. We attack before this Viktor asshole makes another move. Before he reaches Maisy.

I meet their eyes. "We end this before it begins."

"That's my boy!" Uncle Leo exclaims. "Colletti, let's go. We gotta tell the others."

KAI

By the time Uncle Leo and Uncle Colletti have left, I'm on my third glass of whiskey. It's the only thing keeping me from putting my fist through the nearest wall. For fuck's sake!

We hit first. That's it. That's all that matters.

Orion and Logan are sitting on the couch, discussing next steps, when the intercom rings. Without much thought, Logan shoots to his feet and strides over to the elevator where the security camera is.

He glances at it and his expression shifts. There's something on the little screen that's holding his attention. "Who the fuck is this...?" he mutters to himself, and pushes the intercom button.

The voice is clear on the loudspeaker. "Um, boss, someone's here to see you."

"Yeah?" Logan responds.

"Someone called Viktor...Mro-zov-ski. He says you'll wanna see him."

Did I just hear that correctly? My grip tightens around the glass in my hand. I down it in one before slamming it onto the table, the force of it rattling through my bones. "I'll kill him."

I walk over to Logan's side to check the screen myself while Orion leans forward in his seat, his eyes narrowing. He speaks without blinking. "No, you won't."

"Send him up. No guns, just him," Logan says into the intercom.

I snap my head toward him. "Are you out of your goddamn mind?"

"Kai, cool off. He's here to negotiate," Orion says, too assured for my liking.

"Are you telling me that we won't kill him the moment he shows his face?" I demand. "Come on! Don't be so stupid! Can't you see this is our opportunity?"

"Kai, we're not gonna gun him down like cowards," Logan says.

I breathe hard through my nose, trying to steady the rage curling in my gut. I want to fight. I need to fight.

The elevator pings, and Viktor Mrozovski, the culprit who's been disrupting all our lives, steps into the penthouse like he owns the damn place. He's tall and broad-shouldered, dressed in a tailored black suit, with blond hair slicked back in a ponytail. His presence is calculated, controlled.

Logan crosses his arms, using his extra height to leer down at him. "The infamous Viktor Mrozovski."

"So you've heard of me." Viktor smirks, looking completely unfazed.

"You killed quite a lot of our men." Orion's voice is deeper, darker.

I smack a punch into my palm. "We should retaliate right here, right now, Orion."

Viktor's gaze flicks between us, assessing, measuring. Then he exhales, as if bored. "And your fiancée? She's not here to greet me? What a shame," he muses, his voice laced with mock disappointment. "I really wanted to meet her."

The room turns electric.

Logan takes a step closer, his lip curling in barely restrained anger. "You're talking a lot of shit for a man standing in the middle of our turf."

Viktor looks amused. "Am I? Or am I exactly where I need to be?"

I grind my teeth. "You smug—"

Orion holds up a hand, silencing me before I can get blood spilled too soon. He doesn't take his eyes off Viktor. "Leave her out of this."

Viktor tilts his head, considering the request like it's something humorous. Then he shakes his head. "See, that's the problem. I can't leave her out of this." His voice lowers, turning cold. "As long as she's alive, the real Slavs, i.e., myself and my brothers, can't rule. And I'm not about to play nice just because you asked."

My body is already moving before I can stop myself. I step toward him, my fists curling, but Orion shoves an arm in front of me.

Viktor watches, looking unimpressed. "Touchy, aren't we?" His tone is aloof. "I came to give you a warning."

"We don't need your warnings," Logan snaps.

"Oh, but you do," Viktor says, his smirk fading. "You either give her to me, or—"

"New York is ours," I cut in, my voice rough. "You better get your men out if you don't want them to end up in a ditch."

Viktor's expression barely shifts, but what I see in his eyes is amusement. No—pity. The fuck?

He straightens his cuffs and looks at me, then at Logan and Orion. "Someone's ending up in a ditch," he mutters. "That's for sure."

He walks back to the elevator and the door closes behind him, leaving us on edge, primed for war. All because of Maisy. Again.

Orion places his hand on Logan's shoulder. "Call your contact in Chicago. Tell them to call us the moment she lands."

Logan picks up his cell, but it buzzes at that very moment. He brings it to his ear without hesitation. "Martin," he says, glancing between Orion and me. "Tell me."

I don't move. Every second drags, heavy with anticipation.

Logan exhales slowly and nods. "Good." He hangs up and nods at us. "They've gone through security. They're safe."

Relief washes over me. Across from me, Orion

drags a hand over his face. If I didn't know him any better, I'd say he's just as shaken as I am.

"That's one problem solved," he says. But I see the truth in his clenched jaw and rigid shoulders—he's barely keeping it together.

Logan doesn't waste time. He dials again, on speaker. I know exactly who he's calling.

"Rosa," Logan says, his voice lower now, "They should land in a few hours. You know what to do."

I hear Rosa's voice through the speaker, calm and unwavering. "I know, Logan. I'll send my driver to pick them up. They'll be safe. I promise you."

The veins in Logan's neck visibly tighten. "Maisy and the kids are the most precious thing I have. My life is in your hands. And I'll owe you forever."

Rosa sighs softly. "I've got them, Logan. They'll be safe with me."

"Call us the moment they arrive at your house," Orion barks. He doesn't know Rosa, but he's after any semblance of control, no matter how ridiculous.

"Who's that?" comes Rosa's voice unexpectedly. Women usually cower under Orion's demands, but she questions him.

"Orion Carte."

"I'll call the moment they arrive, Orion. Sending your family far away from home must feel daunting. But I got them. You can trust me."

"If Logan trusts you, I do too." Orion nods at Logan to take over. He's satisfied by her answer. And so am I.

"Talk to you soon, Rosa." Logan hangs up, shoving the cell into his pocket.

The tension in the room doesn't ease off.

"We need to assume Viktor knows she's gone," Orion says, first meeting my eyes, then Logan's. "We end this before he ever gets a chance to touch her."

Logan nods slowly. "We have a small window before he realizes she's out of reach."

I crack my knuckles. "Just say when."

CHAPTER 10

MAISY

Georgina's been instrumental in the running of the club this past year, her connections making the impossible possible. It's ironic that while she's been achieving so much, Benji, her Vitali boyfriend, sees her as nothing more than decoration.

I reach Yonkers in good time; the condo she found me is on the northern edge of the city—close enough to stay connected, but still comfortably removed. She'd describe it to her buyers as a sleek, modern, discreet first-floor unit.

"I'm sorry I'm late. I had to make sure I wasn't

followed." I step up to her, glancing up at the building. "This place is secure?"

"It should be." She hands me the key. "I'm selling it, but you can use it for at least a month. No one's around to be asking questions."

I take the key. "Appreciate it."

Georgina exhales, tilting her head to one side. "You want to tell me what the hell's going on?"

"Best if I don't."

"Figured." She watches me for a moment. "Look, whatever you're planning, just be careful. The people we deal with don't leave loose ends."

I grip the key tighter. "I'm not a loose end."

"No," she agrees, and titters. "You're the problem."

I smirk. "Damn right."

"Let me know if you need anything else. I gotta go."

"Sure." I hesitate before speaking again. I know the unwritten rule we have about privacy at the club still stands, but I want to reiterate it. "Georgina, please don't—"

"Don't worry. I was never here," she says, her hand brushing my arm. She holds my gaze for a second longer, then turns and heads to her car.

The moment I step inside the building, relief washes over me. The place is empty—it's just me here.

I enter the condo, lock the door, and lean back against it, letting my shoulders relax. A long, tired breath slips out, one I feel like I've been holding since I left the airport.

I cross the room slowly and look around. Everything feels too big. The high ceilings and bare walls stretch around me.

I lower myself onto the couch, not so much sitting as collapsing, the cushions swallowing me up. All this space feels...off. It's too empty. It's too quiet to be alone with my thoughts, and too late to outrun them.

I take slow breaths, pushing the feeling aside. I can't afford it. Not now. Fuck, I hate this. I hate being alone again.

Next to the couch, I see a panel of buttons. I press one to close the curtains, and within seconds, the daylight is cut off. Almost instantly, the darkness and silence remind me even more of how I used to live. How many nights did I spend alone before I met the men who gave me my life back? Before they nearly died—a few times, too—in order to protect me.

Well, it's time I paid them back.

I've changed over the last few years, I know— where I once cowered in the face of fear, now I stand my ground. With Orion, Logan, and Kai by my side, I'm now thinking more like a Carte, a Vitali, and a Delgado. Having experienced what it means to be saved, and especially now I have my children, I'm beginning to clearly understand the power of protection. I'd rather die protecting my men and my family than run and hide, like I did before. And if that means doing things I'm not going to be proud of, so be it.

I take off my cap, tip my head back, closing my eyes as my thoughts race uncontrollably. I press my palm flat against my chest, feeling the steady beat of my heart, grounding myself. The universe needs to give me a sign. A direction. A clue. Anything.

"Please, God...Mom...Rebecca," I whisper, feeling desperate, "if you're listening, I could use a sign."

My children's faces float through my mind, innocent and trusting. They believe their mom can fix anything, protect them from any monster. I think of Orion, Logan, and Kai—how they'll react when they find out I went against their orders.

And then, I hear it. The sign. A loud bang and a splintering of wood. My heart lurches into my throat as heavy footsteps thunder through the condo. Male voices, speaking in low tones.

My body moves before my brain can catch up. I run to the end of the hallway and into the bedroom, and scan the room desperately for somewhere, anywhere to hide. The closet's too obvious. Behind the curtains? No, that's worse. Under the bed is my only option, pathetic as it is. I slide onto the floor and crawl underneath it, trying to control my panicked breathing.

"Come out, come out, wherever you are," a gruff voice calls out, and my blood turns to ice. "We know you're here, Maisy."

The sound of heavy boots gets closer. I hear them enter the bedroom, and they circle the bed like wolves. I can see their shoes from my hiding spot—expensive Italian leather, because of course these bastards would wear designer shoes to a kidnapping.

"Check under the bed," one of them says with a laugh. They all speak with a hard Eastern European accent. "That's where they always hide in the movies."

My heart stops as a face appears, upside down, and steel-gray eyes meet mine. All I can tell is that he's a predator. "Well, what do we have here?"

I fling out a fist and punch the face in front of me, just before rough hands grab my ankles and drag me out.

"That tickled," the man I hit jeers.

I kick and thrash, but it's useless against their strength. Four men surround me. "Let me go, assholes!" I scream.

"Fuck, Viktor, I didn't know she was so energetic!" a man with biceps bigger than my head chuckles.

Viktor! I have a name. They all look like they're cut from the same cloth: tall, broad-shouldered, dressed in three-piece suits that scream danger. But Viktor's the one who makes my skin crawl with that cold, assessing stare.

"Let—me—go!!" I shout, hating how my voice trembles.

The third one, an intelligent-looking man with a goatee, but intimidating nevertheless, dangles my cell in front of my face. "Not very smart for a genius, are you? Left your cell on. Might as well have sent us an invitation."

The men laugh.

"Don't be so stupid! I switched off my cell!" I retort, still thrashing about.

"Yeah, but not before we pinged you at the airport." He jeers.

"Kill her now," the fourth one says. He looks like he's in charge. "We came to eliminate a threat, not play games."

Viktor's hand shoots out, grabbing the man's throat. "Know your place," Viktor snarls. "I make the decisions around here." His eyes rake over me, and I feel naked despite having on a dress that comes to my knees. "Besides, look at her. Those eyes, that face. She's wasted on those American dogs. We could have some fun first."

"The pretty ones always scream the loudest," the bicep guy says with a grin, revealing teeth set in an ugly, unnatural way.

I try to run away, to slip out of their grip, but together with the bicep guy, Viktor has my arm clamped like his hand is made of iron. "Don't bother running, Maisy-Moo. You're coming with us. Maybe if your men behave, we'll send you back in one piece."

"My name is Maisy Slavinovich," I say through clenched teeth, "and you'll die for this." My heart is thumping in my throat, but my chin is still raised. "All of you will die!" I yell for good measure.

Viktor and the men laugh as I'm preparing to insult them some more, but something hard strikes the back of my head and darkness swallows me whole.

LOGAN

I trust Rosa with my life, but just one more time, I have to reassure myself of this fact.

My fingers hover over her contact on my cell. I want her to respond to me immediately, but she's taking her time, which drives me crazy.

Once a stripper at my father's club, Rosa was more of a mother to me than anyone else. She took me to school in the early years, and those memories of her are fond ones. I can still remember the scent of her perfume, vanilla, as she'd sneak me candy in the morning.

When Maisy had the twins, I just had to find Rosa and find out what had happened to her. Kids do that to you—make you relive your own childhood.

She lives in Chicago now, as Rosa Jakores. The moment she told me, the name brought back vague memories of a tall man in a tailored suit, standing in my father's shadow—until one day, he wasn't. What happened to him, I didn't know at the time, but now I do: Basim Jakores married Rosa and left New York. She told me they'd wanted to build a new life, far from the blood-soaked streets of New York. But Vitali is not a name you can just delete from your background.

"Logan?" comes Rosa's warm voice on the line. "Is everything okay?"

"Hi, Rosa. Yes, all is good. I just wanted to talk to you again."

There's a rustling sound at her end. "Stop worrying. The guest rooms are ready—we'll put the boys in one room, and the girls in the other. Maisy and Sasha will sleep in the same room. And I've already vetted a nanny who can help while they're here."

"Rosa, about the security—" I start, but she doesn't let me finish.

"It's state of the art, Logan. CCTV covering every angle, motion sensors, armed response. Basim made sure of that. Your family will be safer here than they would in Fort Knox," she assures me.

No matter what she says, guilt still gnaws at me. And a deep sense of responsibility. Not just to Maisy and the children, but to Orion and Kai. They also trusted me with this. "Thank you, Rosa. I'm not sure what we would've done without you."

"Logan." Her voice turns stern. "Focus on what's going on over there. And just know that I will protect your family with my life. I promise you that."

I close my eyes. "I can't lose them, Rosa."

"And you won't. My driver will pick them up from the airport—ex-special forces, thoroughly vetted. They'll never be alone, not for a second."

"Thank you, Rosa. For everything."

"You know what I think?" There's a smile in her voice now. "That girl of yours made you better than your father ever was. Better than any of us thought possible."

The truth in her words hits hard. Maisy did save me, in more ways than one.

"Thank you," I say, my resolve strengthening. "And Rosa? Keep them close."

"Like they're my own, Logan. Now go do what you need to do. We'll take care of the rest."

CHAPTER 11

LOGAN

My hand tightens around my cell as Rosa's voice comes through the loudspeaker.

"The kids landed."

There's a pause, too long, too unnatural. My pulse hammers in my ears. Orion, standing by the window, stiffens. Kai, sprawled on the couch, stops swirling the whiskey in his hand.

I don't ask. I demand. "And?"

Another pause.

Rosa exhales. "Maisy wasn't on the flight."

My whole body goes rigid, almost hard, like metal. My fingers flex around the cell before I set it down on the table. "Say that again."

"They boarded at JFK. Everyone but Maisy."

Kai sets his drink down on the table. I'm certain it's because he's tempted to smash the glass.

Orion's eyes meet mine. "What the hell has happened to Maisy?" he growls.

I can barely hear him over the pounding in my head. My thoughts fracture, rearrange, and settle into one singular truth—Maisy is missing. We don't know where the hell she is.

Orion's voice is sharp enough to cut. "Who was the last person to see her?"

Rosa hesitates. "...Sasha said she said her goodbyes and walked out."

I brace my hands on the table, grounding myself before I shatter something.

Kai doesn't have the same restraint. He picks his glass back up and it flies, smashing against the far wall, whiskey dripping down the matte black paint like blood. "You mean to tell me she fucking disappeared in a goddamn airport?" he yells.

"She planned this," Orion says, his grip on his glass almost tight enough to crack the crystal. "She wanted us to know she's in control."

Control. Maisy has always been two things— brilliant, and reckless. And right now, she's out there alone, playing a game none of us understand.

"She didn't disappear," Rosa says. "Angelina and

Celina must know where she is."

The weight in my chest shifts. It's not relief. It's something heavier, and sharper, slicing through my patience.

"What the fuck do you mean?" Orion demands through gritted teeth.

"...Angelina and Celina are here, with Sasha and the kids," Rosa responds reluctantly. "They say they'll stay with us until they need to. They must know where Maisy is."

It feels as if we are in a war zone of silence, the tension thick enough to suffocate all of us. "Put Angelina and Celina on the line," I say.

Rosa takes a deep breath. "Logan—"

"Now."

A beat later, the rustling of movement filters through the speaker. Then Angelina's voice, cool and steady, fills the room. "I'm here."

Celina's follows. "Me too."

I don't waste time. "Where is she?"

"We don't know," Angelina says bluntly.

"Bullshit! Where the fuck did she go?" Orion barks, clearly unable to rein himself in. "You better start talking. Both of you!"

Celina exhales loudly, but she doesn't lose her cool. "Maisy told us to stay with the kids. We're just following orders."

"Her orders mean nothing if she's dead," Kai snaps.

Angelina's tone remains unshaken. "She's not dead."

"You don't know that," I fire back.

She doesn't yield. "I know Maisy. She's survived worse. And she did this to protect you."

My jaw tightens, rage boiling beneath my skin. "For fuck's sake! We don't need her protection!"

"Maybe not," Angelina replies, seemingly unbothered by my hostility. "But the kids do."

Orion's patience snaps. "You're both coming to New York. Immediately."

"We're not leaving the kids. They know us. They trust us. You'd rather they're alone with strangers?" Celina demands.

Rosa's voice cuts in. "They're right, Orion. The kids know them."

My chest is heaving. I want to fire my blades at someone right this very moment. Nothing is going as planned. I'm angry, in shock, and so goddamn powerless.

Angelina's voice lowers, softer but just as sharp. "Go. Find Maisy. Do what you need to do. We'll be here."

The line goes dead.

"They know everything," Kai snaps.

"Of course they do," I scoff.

Orion slams his fist against the table, the sound echoing around the room. "This isn't a fucking game. She's out there, alone, and no one knows where the hell she is?"

"I'm done with this shit," Kai growls. "One minute, she's here, the next, she's gone. And in between all that, I'm betting it'll be us—once again—putting our asses on the line for her. It's like she doesn't give a damn about what it costs us."

ORION

Too many hours have passed, and we have nothing.

"She's not picking up," Logan grinds out. "She's turned off her cell."

"She killed every damn signal," I snap, leaning over the laptop. My jaw is tight, my eyes locked on the airport feed which we managed to get hold off thanks to a few of our men and their extortion skills.

We've been looking through hours of footage, searching every shadow and face in and outside of JFK. It's like looking for a needle in a haystack.

"There. Got her." I jab my finger at the screen, finally relieved. "Let me zoom in."

There she is—Maisy. My stomach twists at the sight. She has a cap on, lips pressed into a thin line. Walks fast, determined.

I scroll the footage frame by frame until the camera catches her from the side. She's lifting her phone, her face unreadable.

I narrow in.

"Who does she call?" Logan squints at the screen.

"Does it say... Georgina?" Kai asks.

The name Georgina clearly flashes on Maisy's screen as the call connects.

I grit my teeth. "Do we know who she is? Where does she live?"

Logan and Kai shake their heads.

"Then let's find the fuck out!" I yell.

I don't wait, I pick up my cells and start dialing. Kai and Logan follow suit. I don't think calling Angelina or Celina would make a difference. They would not give us any information about Georgina.

I call Uncle Leo, he wouldn't know who Georgina is, or where she lives, but I'll ask him to spread the word. She must be found out by the end of day, no matter what.

Kai and Logan talk to their men too. My jaw

aches from how hard I'm clenching it. Maisy slipped through our fingers, and we didn't even see it.

It's a good few hours before I think of calling my sister. Lisa. I call her—not because I expect anything, but because we're running out of options. She answers on the first ring.

"Orion?"

"I need anything you've got on someone called Georgina. A phone number. An address. Whatever you have." I shoot. I don't fucking have the patience for pleasantries. Not when Maisy's life is at stake.

There's a pause. Then papers rustling. "Sure. Hang on... I keep notes for the club. We have a Georgina coming there, if that's the person you're after. Contacts, attendance logs, emergency details—Maisy insisted we be organized."

Of course she did.

"Why do you need this?"

"It's none of your God damn business, Lisa!" I snarl.

She doesn't flinch. Keeps going like I didn't just bite her head off. "I have her work address. And—wait—yes. I noted a personal number. Looks like she filled it out during the last committee update."

She sends it within seconds. Then, another message follows.

Found her home address, too. I'll send it now.

It hits me all at once. The stupidity of it. The blindness.

Why the hell didn't I call Lisa sooner? She was right there. A woman Maisy trusted enough to help run the goddamn backbone of her club.

And I didn't even think of her.

I'm supposed to be the one who sees every angle. Who predicts every threat. And I overlooked my sister, the woman who probably knows more about the club's inner workings than any man.

I underestimated her. No—we all did.

Maisy tried to show us that.

"I got an address!" I nod at Logan and Kai, and we're on the move within minutes.

By the time we reach her sleek Manhattan apartment, I don't bother with the doorbell. I pound until the door creaks under the force. Logan stays two steps back. Kai's arms are crossed, he knows he's not supposed to hit a woman, but I can feel the restraint burning through him.

The door swings open and a drunken man shows up — hair a mess, shirt half-untucked, reeking of whiskey. Logan stiffens the second he sees him. "You've got to be kidding me! Benji?"

Benji blinks at us, squinting like we're too loud for his hangover. "What... what's going on?"

"You didn't report in?" Logan snarls. "Uncle Jon put out the message hours ago. Where the hell have you been?"

Benji's eyes widen like it just clicked. "I didn't check my phone—I—I was out—"

A woman appears behind him in the hallway, pushing gently past. She's dressed immaculately, her face composed, unreadable. This must be Georgina.

"Where is she?" My voice is low and lethal. I could end her right here if she wasn't the only thread leading to Maisy.

"I don't know." Her lie is smooth. Almost believable.

Kai steps forward. "Stop lying."

"Who are you looking for?" Benji slurs. "Tell them the truth, you whore!" He shoves her behind.

Georgina doesn't flinch. "She hasn't contacted me."

I step into her space, close enough for her to feel the threat in my breath. "If Maisy dies, you're as good as buried. And I won't make it quick."

There is a moment of deliberation before she exhales. Her mask slips just a bit. "I don't know where she is right now."

We don't move. We don't blink. We just watch

her squirm, letting the silence tighten like a noose until she starts talking.

She crosses her arms, defensive. "She didn't tell me everything. She only said she needed a safe place to lie low for a while."

My patience snaps. "And you gave it to her?"

Her voice shakes now. "Yes. I found her a condo. Northern Yonkers. It's quiet. New build. Barely furnished. No one's supposed to be there."

Logan's jaw clenches. "Address. Now."

With trembling fingers, Georgina writes it down.

As we turn to leave, Logan's glare pins Benji in place.

"Sober up," he says coldly, stepping closer. "You're Vitali. You don't get to disappear when the families need you. Uncle Jon's not the only one who noticed."

Benji swallows hard as Logan turns and we all walk out.

The drive to Yonkers takes forever. Every red light drags. I've got one hand clenching my knee, the other twitching near my holster. We don't speak. There's nothing left to say.

When we finally pull up, the condo appears at the edge of a quiet, tree-lined street—too quiet. Too perfect. Too clean. Like someone scrubbed the scene before we got here.

The moment I lay eyes on it, I draw my gun. Logan slips out his blades in silent, fluid motion and Kai's already formed his hands into fists.

The place looks undisturbed at first glance, just another boxy brick unit with spotless windows and a trimmed hedge. But then we see it—the front door hanging awkwardly on its frame, the wood splintered and cracked near the lock.

Whoever came through didn't bother with waiting for it to open. This sets my every nerve on edge. My grip tightens on the gun. Whatever this is—we're already too late for part of it.

Someone left in a hurry or didn't plan to stay long.

Kai's ahead of me, sweeping left. Logan goes right. My breath stays shallow, my steps silent.

Inside, I can almost smell the soft scent Maisy always wears. She was definitely here. There is no sign of a fight. No blood. No shattered glass.

Logan steps into the living room and stops. "Orion."

I cross over.

It's there on the armrest of the couch. Her cap. The one she wore at the airport.

Black, curved brim, folded slightly on the edge. I remember her tucking her curls into it on the CCTV footage.

We all know what that means. Someone was here after her.

Maybe minutes. Maybe hours. But the open door tells me one thing with certainty.

We're not the first to find this place.

We leave the house angry, thinking of the worst.

Every step back to the car feels heavier than the last. My thoughts spiral, if they touched her—if they did anything to her— I will rip this city apart, brick by brick, until I find them.

One thing that keeps me from losing it completely is that my children are safe. That's the only thing I hold onto right now.

As for Maisy, we'll figure it out. The condo had cameras. Exterior, possibly street-facing. Maybe even hallway feeds we can tap through the building's system.

There's no clean exit from this. We'll find out who it was. Although deep down, we already know.

MAISY

Cold. That's the first sensation that pierces through the fog in my mind. That and the smell.

I don't know how long I've been in here, but I sense my arms stretched above my head, and my wrists bound to what feels like a metal bedframe. Similar restraints bite into my ankles. I open my eyes, squinting into the shadows. Thin strips of light filter through the edges of a door, barely illuminating the room.

The smell hits me hard—damp, rotten, and sour. It turns my stomach and makes my head spin. And just like that, the memories come rushing back. I feel Logan's torture all over again—the pain, the fear, every second burned into my mind like it happened yesterday. And then there's Marina. Her death left me with a huge scar. I don't think I ever really got over any of it.

A shiver runs through me, and in that moment, it hits me—I can never escape my past. No matter what happens, it's always there, waiting in the dark, ready to pull me back in. And just like that, the adrenaline surges like a warning I can't ignore.

Breathe, Maisy. Think. You've been in this situation before. Helpless. You've turned worse situations around. You can do it again—stay calm, find a way, and survive.

"Hey!" I scream, my voice bouncing off the walls. "Let me out of here!"

The sound of multiple footsteps approaches. Keys jangle, the lock turns, and the fluorescent lights flicker to life. Viktor Mrozovski fills the doorframe, and the other three men I met cluster behind him: fair, tall, and broad.

Their eyes roam all over my body, and that's when I become aware of the fact that with my legs spread open where my feet are bound, my dress has ridden up to my hips, fully exposing my panties.

"Well, well... Sleeping Beauty finally wakes!" The guy with the thick arms lets out a mocking laugh.

"You had us worried, Maisy." Viktor's eyes are cold, almost unhuman. "For a moment, we thought you might sleep through the fun."

"How long have I been in here?" I demand.

Viktor steps closer, a smirk ghosting his face. "Why? Planning to be somewhere else?"

The way they're all leering at my body makes my skin crawl. They're talking to me but their eyes never leave my body.

I force my voice steady. "Look," I say, willing them to meet my eyes. "We can work something out. I can get you a line to the mafia heads. There's no need for this."

He leans down and his breath, laced with the sharp bite of cigarettes, ghosts across my face. The other men snicker behind him. I pull against my restraints, the metal biting into my flesh.

"The great Maisy Slavinovich. The genius. The

survivor." His fingers slide along my thigh, creeping toward the edge of my panties. I jerk my leg, trying to shake him off, but he doesn't stop. "Not so brilliant now, are you?" he sneers.

Horror courses through me as more tall, broad men file into the room, all clearly from his part of the world. Their eyes crawl over my restrained body like insects, hungry and predatory. One of them turns to Viktor.

"Can we have a go at her?"

My stomach lurches as everyone looks at Viktor, waiting for permission like well-trained dogs.

"Sure, cop a feel, let's see how she'll take it," Viktor sniggers as he pulls out his cell and dials a number, stepping back.

At least ten of them storm the room, which is now crowded, with Viktor's men up front, and they start groping me. Screaming would be pointless—no one would hear me, and even if they did, no one would come. My heart pounds so fast it feels like it might tear through my chest. I can't breathe. I can't think. My eyes fill with tears, blurring everything, but I don't dare blink. I'm frozen, trapped in my own body, and my fear is so thick it's choking me.

Tears spill from the corners of my eyes, hot and silent, sliding down my cheeks as I finally slam my lids shut. If I can't see it, maybe I can pretend I'm somewhere else. Maybe, just for a second, I can forget where I am...and what's happening to me. But I know it's hopeless—I sense their rough hands pulling my dress above my chest, and different mouths lowering to my breasts, sucking my nipples, licking, biting, pulling with their teeth. My knees are spread open as far as they'll go, my panties pulled aside, and there are fingers exploring my cunt. I feel hands stroking my legs, my inner thighs, my butt cheeks, fingers exploring my asshole, and much too much skin-to-skin sensation, priming me for something vile.

"Yeah, oh fuck, she's wet!" someone exclaims.

"Viktor, look! Her cunt's crying for us!" They laugh, insert more fingers inside me, and rub my clit. They want me to get aroused. My nub is already swollen, I can feel it.

"Stop it! You sick bastards—you're gonna fucking regret ever touching me! I swear to God, I'll kill you myself!" I yell, hoping to get Viktor's attention. He looks right at me, still on his call, that vile smile curling his lips as he speaks into the cell.

There's nothing I can do—nothing but sit with the weight of my own mistake, feeling so, so stupid because I put myself here. With my eyes closed, there's only one thing I can control: my mind. And I cling to it desperately. I build walls, imagine my escape—but my body is betraying me. It trembles, it aches as I try to swallow the rising panic, because showing fear is the only thing worse than feeling it. But even in my head, I can't fully get away.

"Fucking cunt, she's good for one thing only!"

I half-open my eyes and see the goatee guy unbuckling, his cock jutting out of his pants, and three, four more men doing the same. Viktor's still on the phone, looking uninterested, while I have around eight men ready to fuck me, their knees on the bed already.

Just as I think my world is collapsing on top of me, I hear Viktor's voice, almost like a lifeline in the chaos. "No one touches her!" he growls as he places his cell in his pocket. "If anyone's fucking her, it's gonna be me. Before I end her."

"Fuck you, Vik!" the goatee complains as he rubs his cock on my inner thigh. "Let me have a go just this one time, brother!"

Brother?

Viktor just throws him a glance, and the goatee backs off. Thank God!

With everyone grumbling and griping over their unfulfilled wishes, some of them still with their hands on my body, I force myself to make use of this moment of reprieve.

"Why New York?" The words tumble out. I'm desperate, grasping for anything. "Who told you it was up for grabs?"

Viktor's pale eyes fix on mine. He's amused. "You know you cannot buy yourself any more time than you already have."

"Twenty-five percent of New York is mine." I try to jerk away from the touch of a few hands that are still groping me. Fortunately, they back off.

"I know that very well." His voice drips with smug satisfaction. "And with you dead, I'll rebuild the Slav family from the ashes."

"I'm your fastest way to the top. I know the names, the deals, the secrets. Use me, and you'll win. Kill me, and you'll never get New York."

"You think you have anything left to bargain with?" he laughs, shaking his head like I'm nothing more than a bad joke.

"Someone's feeding you bad information, Viktor." My voice steadies as I find my rhythm. I called him by his name. Our brains are wired to respond to our names; it creates a subtle bond and we are more likely to listen, and to agree.

Viktor studies me for a long moment, then barks out more laughter that echoes off the walls. "You really think you'll get away with it, don't you?" He leans down, his breath hot against my ear. "That brilliant mind of yours won't help you this time! This time, Maisy-Moo, there's no escape."

The other men shift restlessly in the background,

disappointed predators denied their prey. But I barely register them now. My focus narrows on Viktor, on the ice in his eyes and the subtle tells that appeared in his expression when I mentioned his bad intel.

But before I can push further, Viktor straightens, adjusting his suit. "We're done here." He gestures to one of his men. "Make sure she stays secure."

He and most of the others file out one by one, and I see the man with the large biceps nodding slightly at the one with the goatee. The goatee slams the heavy door shut and clicks the lock with devastating finality, leaving me alone with the bicep guy and my racing thoughts.

He's about six-foot-two. Muscular build beneath the expensive black suit. The sleeves of his suit jacket must have been adjusted to the size of his biceps. Blond hair, cropped military style.

"Where am I?" I demand as he circles the bed like an animal. One thing I've learned in my life is that if I don't speak up, I let them decide on the next step. And I'll be damned if I do that. "You always this chatty, or am I getting special treatment?"

He pauses mid-stride, his eyebrows lifting a fraction. A micro-expression of surprise. Good. He expected fear, not sass. Fear I have in spades, but right now, fear won't save me.

"American women," he says in his strange

accent. "Always talking."

I smile, the kind that I know never reaches my eyes. "Actually, I'm an excellent listener. Why don't you start? Your name would be nice."

The corner of his mouth twitches. Not quite a smile, but close. "Igor. And you're in Washington DC. Not that it matters."

One small victory. "Nice to meet you, Igor. Do you know how long I have been in here?"

"Two whole days. We hit your head harder than we should have."

"I'm a tough nut to crack, Igor." I smile. "I'm Maisy."

"I know who you are." He resumes circling, but slower now. More deliberate. "Maisy Slavinovich. The genius girl who plays with the New York dogs."

The thought of Orion, Logan, and Kai sends a pang through my chest. "And you're Viktor's brother?" I ask casually. I need more information.

He nods.

"How many of you are there? Three? Four? You, Viktor, and...remind me of the others' names?"

"Zoran, he's the one with the goatee." Igor snorts. "He thinks it makes him look tough."

"And the fourth?"

"Dejan. The youngest."

Viktor, Igor, Zoran, Dejan. Four Slavs, with

resources and guns.

"You're a long way from home," I say. "Where is that exactly? Russia?"

His face darkens. "North Macedonia. Skopje." He pronounces it with pride. "Not that Americans know the difference."

"I do, actually." My photographic memory flashes through images of maps and geopolitical histories. "Beautiful country. Torn by corruption and nepotism. Economic struggles recently."

Something shifts in his eyes—recognition, maybe. The realization I'm not just another pretty face.

"Is that why you came here? Economic opportunity?"

Igor laughs. "You could say that."

He sits on the bed next to me, which makes my heart jump into my throat. I have to be focused. "Must be an adjustment," I say. "Washington's a long way from Skopje."

"Washington is just temporary," he says. His fingers start trailing along my leg, from the ankle up. "New York is the prize." He's not even looking at me. He's focused on my leg.

My stomach tightens. "New York's taken," I say carefully.

Igor smiles, showing teeth. "Not for long. Your men—they are soft. Americans." He spits out the word.

"Viktor says you are the brain behind them. Without you..." He makes a dismissive gesture with his hand, removing his vile touch from my skin, but only for a moment.

I force a laugh. "Viktor's giving me too much credit."

"No." He looks at me with interest. "I don't think so. My brother is many things. Stupid is not one of them."

A new tactic, then. "Why New York? Plenty of other cities."

"Viktor wants it." He shrugs as he continues trailing his fingers up my leg. "And what Viktor wants..."

"The brothers provide," I finish. "Family loyalty. I understand that better than most."

His eyebrows rise again. "Do you?"

"I have six children at home. And men who would burn the world to get me back." I say it matter-of-factly, not as a threat. Just the truth. "Tell me about Skopje. About your people there."

"What is there to tell? It's home." His face hardens. "Was home. Now, we are here."

"All of you?" I keep my tone casual. "Your extended family, friends?"

"All who matter." He gestures vaguely, his hand now at my hip. "Viktor brought everyone. There is nothing left for us there."

So the force we are facing is finite. Not an endless stream of reinforcements from overseas, but what they have already brought.

"And why Viktor?" I ask. "Why aren't you leading? You seem capable."

I see a flash of something dangerous in his eyes. "Viktor is eldest. It is tradition."

"Even if you disagree with his methods?"

His jaw clenches. "I did not say this."

I smile softly. "You didn't have to."

We stare at each other, the air between us charged, and I realize I pushed too far, too fast. He must have read my mind because he grins wickedly and pulls a large knife from his pocket.

"Hey! Wait! What are you—" Terrified, I scream and start jerking against my restraints. I'm not ready to die here and now.

Completely ignoring me, Igor hooks his fingers into the waistband of my panties and cuts with the knife. He does it on both sides and pulls them fully off.

"Fuck, yes!!!" He takes them and stuffs them under his nose, inhaling deeply in a perverted, horrific way.

My cries must have been heard, or maybe Viktor realized that Igor was missing, because I hear the sound of footsteps, the lock clicking, and the basement door flying open.

Viktor strides in, every movement containing controlled rage. His eyes lock on mine first, then snap to his brother, who pulls my dress down over my naked cunt in a rush and straightens up.

"What the fuck are you doing here?" Viktor's voice is quiet, which somehow makes it more threatening.

Igor straightens, shoulders squaring. "She had questions."

Viktor steps closer to his brother. "And you gave answers?" Though they are similar in height, Viktor seems to tower over him.

"She knows nothing important," Igor mutters.

"You don't decide what's important." Viktor's voice is ice. "Go upstairs. Deal with other problems."

For a moment, Igor looks like he'll argue. His eyes flick to me, then back to his brother.

"As you wish, brother." He pauses at the foot of the bed, and our eyes meet briefly before he moves toward the door.

"And leave her panties, you freak!" Viktor shouts, which makes Igor throw my cut-up panties onto the bed.

Igor disappears from the room, and Viktor turns to me.

"You can try all you want, but you'll be dead before you know it."

ORION

We've been tearing the city apart for two days straight, hunting for any trace of Maisy.

We have eyes on Ma Molly's house in D.C.— every hour, every shadow, just in case someone's reckless enough to bring her there. But nothing. No movement. No slip-ups.

We hit the streets, chasing down every name, every whisper. We lean on our contacts, we threaten, we torture, we kill. And still, she's gone. It's like she vanished into smoke.

By the time we drag ourselves back to the penthouse on day two, the city is just starting to wake up. The adrenaline that kept us going is almost gone now, burned out and brittle. All that's left is raw nerves, empty rage, and an exhaustion that's begun to rot us from the inside out.

We're running out of leads. And worse—out of time.

Kai drops onto the sofa first, slumping back with

a heavy exhale. Logan heads for the kitchen, pours himself a glass of water he doesn't touch, then walks to the far end of the sofa and sits there, on the opposite end of Kai. I drop in the chair. Elbows on knees. Hands steepled. Thinking.

It's been forty-eight hours and we need sleep. We need to be able to think again. To stop the worst-case scenarios from running on repeat through our heads.

At six in the morning, we're just starting to shut down—each of us slipping into our own spiral—when my phone rings and vibrates against my thigh.

A sharp buzz in the silence. And then ring. Just like that, I'm wide awake.

I pull the cell from my pocket and see an unknown number.

"Carte."

"I hope I'm not interrupting anything important." The voice is thick with an accent. Fucking asshole. It's him.

My blood runs cold. I glance up at Logan and Kai, tap the speaker button, and place the cell on the table. "What do you want, Viktor?"

A low chuckle crackles through the speaker. "I'm calling because I have something of yours."

I'm gonna kill this motherfucker.

"Do you, now?" I try to sound calm but inside, my heart has stopped.

"Yes. Maisy. But you knew that already."

I press my palms flat against the cool table to stop myself from crushing the cell. "If you touch her—"

"Touch her?" Viktor laughs. "I'm afraid we're well past that, Orion. Your little genius isn't as smart as everyone says. Walked straight into my hands like a lamb to slaughter."

Logan moves closer to the phone. "What do you want, Mrozovski?"

"Logan Vitali...I was wondering when you'd join the conversation." Viktor's voice drops an octave. "What do I want? Right now, I'm just enjoying the moment. You should've seen how she fought when my brothers dragged her in."

Kai's eyes lock onto the cell as if it were Viktor's throat.

"She's quite the prize," Viktor continues. "Fertile, too. I think my brothers enjoy her company as we're speaking. Maybe I'll keep her for a few years, you know. I want a bunch of kids from her bloodline. She has a thing for multiple men, doesn't she?"

Kai explodes. "You fucking touch her and I'll rip your throat out with my bare hands! You hear me? I'll fucking kill you myself!"

Viktor's laugh concerns me as much as his words. "I'd be careful, Delgado. Anger clouds judgment, and you'll need all your wits about you if you want to collect what's left of her at some point in the future."

I feel something crack inside me—the devil himself just entered my body. "This isn't a game, Viktor."

"No? Everything is a game, Orion." His voice hardens. "You can collect her body from Hillandale Gate House, Berkley, Washington DC. She'll be quite busy today all day, so perhaps... come in a couple of days? That'll give us sufficient time with her."

The line goes dead, and for a while, none of us moves. Then Kai erupts with a roar, throwing—and breaking—everything he can get his hands on. Logan turns away; I can tell he's trying to contain his rage, but the way he looks, it would frighten anyone approaching him right now.

"He's fucking dead," Kai spits, pacing like a caged animal. "I'm gonna tear him apart."

"We need a plan," Logan says, already moving to the cabinet where he keeps the weapons. "We're not waiting until tomorrow. They might...Fuck! I'm not gonna say it because it ain't happening. Not while I'm still alive!"

My mind shifts into overdrive, analyzing the whole situation. "We need to be smart about this. Viktor's compound is in what used to be Ma Molly's place, and we know that's fortified. Guards at every entrance. Security systems. He wouldn't have told us to go there if he wasn't confident we couldn't get in. Plus, it could be a trap."

"I don't give a fuck," Kai says, grabbing his jacket. "Maisy's in there."

"And we'll get her out," I snap, grabbing his arm. "But not by charging in blind. That's exactly what he wants."

Logan returns, not with weapons but a laptop. His fingers start flying over the keyboard. "Let's look at what we're dealing with. There's a service entrance on the east side with minimal security cameras."

I nod. "He'll expect us to come in with force. Every single person in our syndicate."

"So we don't do what he expects," Logan concludes, eyes never leaving the screen. "We go in small. Just the three of us."

Kai stops pacing, quickly switching from fury to strategy. "Three points of entry. I take the roof. Logan, you take the basement. There's likely an access point through the parking garage." He points to the schematic. "Orion will go through the service entrance. We coordinate by earpiece. Strike simultaneously at midnight."

"Weapons?" Logan asks, already pulling out his medical bag, which I know contains more blades than anything else.

"I'm not sure this is a good idea. I'd rather we have backup," I say, but Kai's already decided.

"Non-lethal for the guards," he rumbles on without acknowledging that I spoke. "We need to move quickly, quietly. Save the bullets for Viktor and his inner circle." He meets my eyes. "This might get personal."

"It's already personal," Logan growls, checking his phone. "I can have Martin bring us night vision gear and flash suppressors in twenty minutes."

They both stop and look at me. "What do you say, Orion?" Kai asks.

I feel the weight of my decision and clench my fists. It's a bad idea, but I agree. "Viktor thinks he knows us. Thinks he can predict our reactions. But he doesn't understand what Maisy means to us."

For men like us, with our complicated, blood-soaked histories, family isn't about DNA. It's about who you'd die for. Kill for.

"We move at dusk," I decide, already reaching for my cell to arrange surveillance on Viktor's building. "Won't call our usual contacts. He'll have ears everywhere."

Kai nods. "When we find her, I get the first shot at him."

"We'll see who reaches him first," Logan says, checking each blade before packing it away.

CHAPTER 12

ORION

After forty-eight hours of nonstop searching for Maisy, instead to resting, we're yet again running on adrenaline and preparing for breaking and entering Viktor's place in Washington DC.

Ten hours have passed since Viktor's call. It's coming close to late afternoon as Logan paces by the windows, and Kai sits at the edge of the couch, wrapping his hands in boxing tape—a ritual he's started to perform lately when preparing to draw blood. I stand at the center of it all, checking my watch for the fifth time in as many minutes.

"The surveillance feed should be up by now," I say, scrolling through my cell for messages. The tech specialist has been working on hacking Viktor's security cameras, but progress is slow. Too slow.

"We're running out of time," Kai mutters, the tape making a ripping sound as he tears it with his teeth.

My cell lights up. I look at the screen. "Unknown number."

The three of us exchange glances. I answer immediately, putting it on speaker. "Carte."

The other end is silent, but I can hear someone breathing.

"Orion."

My breath catches in my throat. Maisy? Not frightened, not broken, not pleading. Just...flat. Cold.

"Maisy? Are you alright? Where are you?" The words tumble out before I can arrange them into something more controlled.

"I'm fine." Her tone is clipped, precise. No emotion. Nothing like the woman who shares our bed, who cradles our children, who matches me word for calculated word. "Better than fine, actually."

Logan moves closer to the phone. "Maisy, are you alone? Can you speak freely?"

A soft laugh, one I've never heard from her before. "Yes, Logan. I'm alone. And speaking very freely."

Kai leans forward, his eyes never leaving the phone. "What's going on, Maisy? What did that Slav do to you?"

"Nothing I didn't want him to do." The statement falls like a blade between us. "That's actually why I'm calling. I need you all to understand something."

My jaw clenches, my rings pressing into my skin as I curl my fingers into fists. "We're listening."

"Twenty-five percent of New York territory is mine." Her voice hardens. "I'm claiming it back. Effective immediately."

The words don't register at first. They simply can't. Not when they come from her.

"What the fuck are you talking about?" Kai demands, already on his feet. "This isn't funny, Maisy."

"I'm not trying to be funny." She sounds almost bored now. "I've made a business decision. I need to think about myself. It's nothing personal."

Logan's eyes meet mine. He knows, as I do, that something is deeply wrong. This isn't Maisy.

"Viktor's forcing you to say this," I state, keeping my voice even. "Whatever he's threatening you with—"

"Viktor isn't forcing me to do anything," she cuts in. "Neither are his brothers. We're partners now. Equals. Something I never quite felt with you three."

The floor seems to shift beneath my feet.

"You expect us to buy that you willingly allied with the Mrozovski brothers?" Logan asks in disbelief. "The same men who've been threatening our territory for months? Who've been killing our people?"

"Yes," she counters. "We come from the same blood. We have common ground. They understand where I come from in a way you three never could."

My mind races, searching for the angle, the play. I know Maisy always has a strategy, but this is something new. Something I've never seen with her.

"What about our children?" I ask. "What about our family?"

A pause. Brief, but telling.

"I've been playing house long enough," she says eventually, her voice hardening again. "I was never meant to be just a mother, just a lover to three men. I was destined for more than that, and it's time I claimed it."

Kai slams his taped fist against the wall. "Bullshit! This isn't you talking, Maisy!"

"You never really knew me, Kai," she replies, ice in every syllable. "None of you did. You saw what you wanted to see—a broken girl you could fix, a genius you could control, a body you could share."

The words strike like physical blows.

"And Viktor?" I ask, forcing each word past the tightness in my throat. "What does he see?"

"A queen." Simple, direct. "Not a possession."

Logan steps closer to the phone, his instincts reading between her words. "Maisy, if you're in danger, if he's watching you—"

"I told you, I'm alone," she snaps. "No one's making me say any of this. I'm finally thinking clearly, for the first time in years."

I close my eyes as she speaks, searching for the tells in her voice, the subtle cues that would signal distress. Instead, I hear only certainty. Cold, hard certainty.

"So that's it?" Kai asks, raw pain bleeding through his anger. "You're just switching sides? Throwing away everything we built together?"

"I built my part," she says, "and now I'm taking it with me. The eastern territories, the docks, the financial district operations—all mine. I expect a smooth transition."

My lawyer's mind catalogs what this would mean. A quarter of our empire, gone. Vulnerable borders. War with the Slavs all but guaranteed.

"You know we can't let that happen," I tell her, my voice dropping to something I've never directed at her before.

"You don't have a choice," she replies, matching my tone, "unless you want an all-out war. And trust me, with what I know about your operations, you'd lose. Badly."

The threat hangs in the air between us. Maisy knows everything—every weakness, every secret, every vulnerability in our organization. She helped build our security, our strategy, our future.

"Why are you doing this?" Logan asks. "The real reason, Maisy."

"I told you. I've outgrown you." Her words are measured, precise strikes. "I'm not asking for permission. I'm telling you how things will be from now on."

Kai's unable to contain his rage, as usual. "So you're fucking the Mrozovski brothers now? Is that it?"

"My personal arrangements are none of your concern anymore, Kai," she says coldly. "But since you asked—not yet. Although I'll let you know the moment I do."

The image this conjures up makes my stomach turn. Not from jealousy, but from wrongness. This isn't Maisy. Not the woman who fought alongside us, who bore our children, who went through hell only a short while ago.

"I don't believe you," I say quietly. "I know you, Maisy Roy."

"You know what I wanted you to know," she counters. "Nothing more."

"What about the children?" Logan asks. "Your children. Our children."

The silence stretches out for longer this time. When she speaks, her voice is firmer, as if she's pushing through something. "They're better off without me. I was never built for motherhood."

And there it is. The first real crack in her performance. Maisy would never abandon her children. Not willingly. Not for power, not for revenge, not for anything in this world.

"We're coming for you," I say, certainty settling into my bones. "Whatever game Viktor's playing, whatever he's forced you to say—it won't work."

"There is no game," she insists, but I hear it now—the smallest tremor in her voice. "I'm making a choice. My choice. Stay away, Orion. All of you. This call is a professional courtesy, nothing more."

"One question," I say, leaning closer to the phone. "Do you remember what you said to me the night the twins were born? When it was just you and me in that hospital room?"

Silence.

"Maisy?" I press.

"I need to go," she says abruptly. "Consider this my formal separation from our arrangement. Any attempt to intervene will be considered an act of war."

The line goes dead.

For several heartbeats, none of us moves. The penthouse feels colder somehow, as if her words have leeched all warmth from the air.

"She must be lying," Kai says, certainty in every line of his body. "Viktor's got her. He's making her say that shit."

Logan nods slowly. "There were inconsistencies. Hesitations. The way she spoke about the children—that wasn't Maisy."

I move to the windows, staring out at the city that's partially ours, partially hers. The city Viktor wants to take.

"She's sending us a message," I say, everything clicking into place. "She's telling us she's with Viktor. She mentioned the brothers. She emphasized being alone in the room."

"She's feeding us what she can," Logan concludes.

"But why tell us to stay away?" Kai asks, confusion warring with hope on his face. "If she wants us to come for her—"

"Because Viktor's planning something," I realize, turning back to them. "The territory claim, the brothers, telling us explicitly to stay away—it's a warning. He wants us to come charging in. It's a trap."

Logan's eyes narrow. "So what do we do? We can't leave her there."

"We don't," I say, resolve hardening in my chest. "But we don't play by Viktor's rules either."

Kai steps forward. "Right. What's the play?"

"Viktor thinks he knows us," I say.

Logan nods, already reaching for his arsenal.

"And they expect us tonight."

"We hit them tomorrow, right in the chaos of morning rush hour," I say, final. "They won't see it coming."

Kai's smile is all teeth, primal and hungry. "I'm gonna enjoy tearing those brothers apart."

MAISY

"That brilliant mind of yours won't help you this time!" Viktor had yelled angrily at me. "This time, Maisy-Moo, there's no escape."

But that didn't stop me. I was watching closely, and for a split second—just a heartbeat—doubt flickered across his features. I saw it the moment I mentioned someone had been feeding him bad information. That he's been played.

The smallest crack in his certainty.

"Make sure she stays secure," he barked as he left the basement.

In a way, it worked in my favor. Igor, Viktor's brother, all biceps and sleaze—turned out to be a talker. A major pervert, unstable and unpredictable yes, but also an easy source of information. If Viktor hadn't walked back when I screamed, I probably would've been raped by him.

Igor was thrown out without a word of explanation, and when the door slammed shut behind him, Viktor came over and released one of my hands. Then my legs. Left just one wrist cuffed to the bed.

The moment my hand was free I pulled my dress down and covered myself, trying to forget the number of hands that were on me only minutes before. I sat on the edge of the bed, waiting to see what was coming next. Certainly not expecting Viktor to save me.

Of course, being the monster he is, he took my pain and twisted it deeper. My stomach lurches at the memory, bile rising in my throat as I recall that horrific video on his cell.

The video was grainy, shot from an odd angle, but clear enough: Angelina and Celina in a park with the kids, laughing, completely unaware they were being recorded. A man's hand entered the frame, stroking Gracie's soft curls, and my little girl, looking up with her trusting smile that breaks my heart.

"You want ice cream, pretty girl?" the man asked in a thick Eastern European accent.

Then Damien—God, my sweet, Damien—jumped into the stranger's lap, shouting that he wanted ice cream too. Angelina and Celina chuckled in the background, oblivious to the predator in their midst.

But what broke me was seeing the man's hand settling on Damien's tiny neck, his thick fingers positioning themselves with precision.

Viktor paused the video just there, his index finger hovering over the screen. "One word," he said, "and his neck will be snapped like a twig."

I threw up right there on the bed, guilt and terror mixing into a toxic cocktail that emptied my stomach and filled my veins with dread.

"W-where are my children?" I choked out, trembling, my voice caught between a sob and the aftertaste of bile.

"Safe... for now." He sneered.

This was my fault. I'd brought this nightmare upon them by ignoring Orion's warnings about security protocols.

Viktor stood there, watching as I vomited until nothing but bitter yellow bile poured from my mouth— and even then, he didn't stop. He kept making his cruel jokes, calling me stupid, mocking how I'd somehow convinced the world I was a genius. Maybe he was right. Maybe I was a fool. But all I could think about at that moment was my children. I had to find a way to save them—no matter what it cost me.

I wiped my mouth with the back of my hand, tasting bile and iron. My throat burned, but I swallowed the last of it down, forcing my head up. Viktor was still there, leaning against the steel frame of the bed like he owned the world, enjoying my humiliation.

His smug grin was revolting. "You really are something, Maisy. A genius, they say. But here you are, puking your guts out like a scared little girl." His words slithered under my skin.

"Even a genius can have a weak stomach," I rasped. "At least I'm still standing."

His pale eyes flashed with something darker. "For now."

I drew in a slow breath, steadying the tremor in my hands. I couldn't let them see the cracks. Not yet. "You win, Viktor," I said. "I was stupid. Too proud. Too...blind. You were right about me."

His grin widened. "Say that again."

"You were right," I repeated, pushing each word past the knot in my throat. "I thought I could play this game, outsmart you. But I was wrong."

Viktor stepped closer and crouched in front of me. "I knew you'd see reason," he murmured. "But it's too late for that, isn't it? Your little empire is crumbling. Orion, Logan, and Kai are holding your leash."

My stomach twisted. Nobody owns me, that's for sure. "That leash is up for the taking," I whispered, casting my eyes down. "And maybe...maybe we could build something stronger together. You, me, your brothers. We could run New York. Split the pie."

I lifted my gaze, willing Viktor to see a spark of ambition beneath my defeat. His breath hitched. Just a fraction. But I caught it.

"You want a seat at my table?" he asked, somewhat skeptical.

I nodded, slow, deliberate. "I give you a quarter of New York. And my help in convincing the Council to accept you. That's your biggest hurdle."

"And why would I trust you?" Viktor finally asked.

I forced myself to hold his gaze. "Because I want to survive. I want my children to survive. And I know the only way to do that is to stand with you."

Viktor rose, towering over me, and for a moment, I saw the monster he truly was. He leaned in, his lips brushing my ear. "You'd betray your lovers for a slice of power?"

"I'm a Slav. What do you think?" I sneered.

His laughter rumbled around the room. "I almost believe you."

I grabbed his wrist. "Let me prove it. Let me talk to the Council. I know some of the men there."

He pulled back, studying me like I was a puzzle he hadn't quite solved. "If you lie, Maisy, if you so much as blink the wrong way—"

"I know," I interrupted, and met his threat head-on. "But I won't."

Viktor's eyes narrowed, weighing me up, testing. Finally, he nodded, a sharp bob of his chin. "You'll stay here. Under my watch. Until the meeting. But right now…" He waved his cell at me. "Call home. Tell them you're not coming back."

I nodded, though my stomach lurched. "You're making the right choice, Viktor," I said as I dialed Orion's number.

KAI

The three of us—Orion, Logan, and I—have spent hours preparing. It's midnight and we're stocking weapons, running through plans, knowing damn well Viktor Mrozovski won't go down easy.

But all of that shatters the second we hear the buzz of the intercom.

It's Uncle Colletti's voice crackling through the speaker, and his words barely make sense. "Maisy's downstairs. Says she wants to come up."

Orion freezes beside me. Logan's head snaps toward the panel like he's misheard. No way. No fucking way.

We rush to crowd around the screen monitor. And there she is. Maisy. Standing in the lobby like she didn't rip out our souls a couple of hours ago. And she's not alone.

The Mrozovski brothers flank her like prison guards. Viktor's hand is glued to her waist, possessive, smug. The rest of them are standing too close to her, looking much too sure of themselves.

I stare at the screen, trying to process what the hell I'm looking at. Orion does too, his jaw clenched so hard I think he might snap a tooth. Logan's expression is pure shock.

He taps the intercom. "We're coming down."

"Fuck, what does this mean?" I ask, not knowing what the hell to expect.

After punching a few buttons, Orion checks the CCTV feed, flicking through the angles outside the building. "See all these parked cars," he says. "It's them. They're out there. Slavs."

I feel my stomach drop. We were all ready to take on Viktor, but now with Maisy right in the middle of it, it's going to be tough.

No matter how much I want to tear Viktor apart with my bare hands, I can't risk her getting caught in the crossfire. In a small space like that lobby? One wrong move, one bullet fired, and Maisy could be the one bleeding out on the floor.

I can feel Logan thinking the same thing. Can see it in Orion's eyes, too. None of us wants to be the one to say it out loud, to give voice to that fear. That whatever game she is playing down there—whether it's real or not—could get her killed before we even understand why.

I stare at that screen, at her face, searching for something. A sign. A signal. Anything that could tell me what the hell she's doing. But all I see is the mask she wears, standing at Viktor's side like she belongs there.

And that's the worst part.

Without a word between us, the moment the elevator doors slide open, we step inside without so much as a hint of a plan.

"Brace yourselves, men," Orion says, his grim voice doing more to prepare us than any warning ever could.

The very moment the doors open, I look past Uncle Colletti and Uncle Leo and I see her. Maisy. Standing in the lobby like a ghost wearing someone else's skin. We move toward her in unison, my pulse thrashing against my ribs, refusing to calm.

There she is. Our Maisy. But she's not alone.

Viktor Mrozovski's hand is still wrapped around her waist like he owns her, and I feel fire igniting in my veins. His touch is a violation. I can barely see straight as my hands clench into fists at my sides.

Her eyes flicker up, meeting mine. Just for a second, I see her. Maisy.

But then Viktor tightens his grip, pulling her closer like he knows exactly how to twist the knife. That possessive smirk curls at the edges of his mouth. I'd like to knock it off his face.

"Get your fucking hands off her!" I roar, lunging forward, my fist already flying.

But I never make it. One of Viktor's brothers steps in, fast as lightning. His fist connects with my jaw with a crack that rocks my skull and drops me to my knees.

The pain flashes bright and hot, but my rage burns hotter at the sound of Maisy's scream. Before I can push myself up, Logan's already moving; there's a flash of silver, and then his blade is embedded deep into the man's unnaturally big bicep. Blood stains the bastard's suit as he roars in pain.

"Fuck!" he shrieks, his face contorting. "You're a dead man, doctor. You're a fucking dead man!"

The lobby explodes into chaos. Orion launches himself at Viktor, landing a vicious blow that snaps his head back. Viktor stumbles but doesn't fall. Orion pulls back for another strike, rage oozing from his usually controlled features.

"Stop!" Maisy throws herself between them, her

hands splayed against Orion's chest. "Don't hurt him!"

With his fist raised, Orion freezes. His eyes lock on hers, and I see confusion twisting into devastation. "Maisy?"

Logan's dragging me to my feet, his hands steady, his gaze never leaving Maisy.

She stands there looking like a stranger: Viktor at her side, his brothers lining up behind him like wolves—even the wounded one—ready to fire their guns.

Uncle Leo and Uncle Colletti draw their weapons, turning the penthouse lobby into a powder keg. This is about to become a bloodbath.

"Enough!" Maisy yells.

The room stills, and men with generations of violence in their blood all turn to stare at her.

For a moment, all I can hear is my own breath, ragged and sharp. She looks at us like we're the enemy. Like she means it.

"It's over," she says, steady and cold. "This thing between us. It's done."

Logan doesn't flinch. "This thing, as you call it, can never be done."

Her face is stone. "I'm a Slav. I've always been a Slav. I was just waiting for the right moment."

I step forward, blood dripping from my split lip, my heart breaking all over again. "Bullshit. This isn't you, Maisy. What has he done to you?"

Her eyes meet mine. "I'm not who you think I am," she says. "I never was. Uncle Leo and Uncle Colletti saw through me a long time ago. Didn't you?"

The two old bastards exchange smug glances, vindication written all over their faces.

Orion's voice comes out barely audible. "All this was a lie?"

Maisy nods, her mask never cracking. "I did what I had to do. I played your game. And now I'm done playing."

Logan's mask, meanwhile, slips. He's not hiding his feelings any longer. "You're making a mistake, Maisy. Whatever he's promised you—"

She cuts him off. "He hasn't promised me anything. At least he's honest about what he is. You three wrapped your violence in pretty packages and expected me to be grateful."

Her words sear. I feel Logan tense beside me, and Orion looks hollowed out. I can't stand it.

"You wanted to own me," Maisy continues, "but you never really knew me."

"That's not true," Orion says. "We loved you—"

Maisy laughs, sharp as broken glass. "You don't love me. You love controlling me. Protecting me. Keeping me. But you never just loved me."

"How can you say that? After everything—" I falter. The pain is too raw.

"After everything, I'm choosing this," she says, gesturing to Viktor and his brothers. "I'm choosing my real family."

I lose my footing from the hit I took, and Logan catches me before I hit the ground again, steadying me, but it doesn't matter. I feel like I've already fallen.

"So that's it?" Logan asks, his voice flat. "You're walking away? From us? From our children?"

Her face hardens. "The children will be fine. They'll understand someday."

Orion's voice slices through the silence. "They will never understand this betrayal. And neither will I."

Viktor smirks, his hand sliding around Maisy's waist again. "I think she's made herself clear, gentlemen. You gotta learn to share New York now. The Slavs are back in town."

Maisy lets him lead her toward the door, her body moving but her eyes are dead. I watch, helpless, as Viktor presses a kiss to her cheek, sealing the betrayal with a final, possessive claim.

At the exit, Viktor turns back. His grin is cruel. "Oh, and I'm still thinking about if I should spare your kids or not. Shall we let them enjoy Chicago a little longer?"

Horror floods my chest. I drop to my knees, Logan crouching beside me, but all I can see is Maisy, walking away from everything we've built. Everything we were.

The door closes behind them, and I feel the world collapse in their wake.

CHAPTER 13

KAI

The penthouse feels like a fucking tomb. My head pounds with each heartbeat, blood rushing in my ears as I pace the floor. I can't process what just happened. Maisy. Our Maisy. The words keep looping: betrayal, Viktor, children, over.

Logan's cell is already pressed to his ear as he stands by the floor-to-ceiling windows overlooking the city. His face may be carved from stone, but I see the tremor in his hand.

I slam my fist against the wall. Pain shoots through my knuckles, but it's nothing compared to the gaping wound in my chest. Maisy knew where to aim. Right at the fucking heart.

"Angelina," Logan says into the phone, his voice controlled despite everything crumbling around us. "Are the children okay?" After a short silence, he exhales. "Good. Now listen carefully. You and Celina need to bring them home immediately."

Orion collapses into a leather chair, elbows on his knees, head hanging. He's never looked so broken. The most powerful man I know, reduced to this.

"You will have to wake them up. If you take the next plane to New York, you'll be here by the morning. And not a word to anyone," Logan continues. "A man called Viktor Mrozovski, a very dangerous man, knows they're in Chicago. I don't know what his next move is, but I'm not taking any chances."

Orion's head snaps up at the mention of Viktor. His eyes are bloodshot, his normally perfect appearance utterly disheveled. "She told him where our children are," he whispers, more to himself than us.

I slide down the wall until I hit the floor, my legs giving out. This feels familiar—this emptiness, this void where everything meaningful used to be. I've been here before, ready to give it all up.

Maisy. Even thinking her name burns.

"No, Angelina, you don't understand," Logan says, his voice rising slightly. "Maisy betrayed everything. Everyone." He pauses to listen for a moment, then says, "Viktor knows where the kids are. She told him. It's over."

His words hang in the air like smoke: it's over. The life we built, the family we created—destroyed by the one person we all trusted completely.

"You're probably being watched," Logan adds. "No one must know you're coming back."

I stare at the ceiling, letting numbness wash over me. Maybe this is better. Maybe I was never meant for happiness, for family, for love. Boxers like me, criminals like me—we don't get happy endings.

"I trust Rosa, so you can tell her, but no one else," Logan instructs. "I'll be waiting for your call about pickup." Another pause. "I don't care what you think, Angelina. I don't give a fuck if you believe me or not. Just get our kids home safely."

He ends the call with a vicious jab of his finger and hurls the phone onto the couch. "They don't buy it," he says flatly. "They trust Maisy more than life itself. Think she must have had a good reason."

"There is no good reason," Orion says, his voice hollow. "Our children. Our fucking children. Betrayed by their mother."

The thought of Viktor—that sadistic fuck— knowing where our children are makes me want to tear the world apart.

"We'll kill him," I say, the words automatic. "Then her."

Before either can respond, the elevator doors ping. Lisa appears, cheeks flushed, eyes wild. "What the hell's happening?" she demands. "I just saw Maisy leaving with someone called...Viktor. What's that all about?"

"Not now, Lisa," Orion snaps, not even looking at her.

Lisa steps further into the room, taking in the state of all of us. "What happened?"

"I said not now!" Orion growls.

She doesn't budge. "No! Tell me."

Logan blocks her path. "We don't want to talk about her."

"Her?" Lisa echoes, confusion evident on her face. "Have you seen her lately? Something was definitely off. Her cell is not working, she hasn't responded to my messages. I mean, aren't you worried?"

I lift my head, studying Lisa's expression. There's genuine concern there.

"She was with someone called Viktor." She shakes her head like she still can't believe what she saw. "Kai, they were surrounding her like she was their captive."

My heart punches into my ribs. "Maybe she wanted to be with him?"

Lisa glares at me like I've lost my mind. "Don't be ridiculous. She tried to play it off—said Viktor was her very close friend. But she was lying. She looked right at me like she wanted to scream.”

Orion finally lifts his head to look at her, her words grabbing hold of something inside him.

“Where the hell have you been, Lisa? It's midnight,” he asks, his tone sharp.

Lisa straightens, brushing her hair behind her ear. “I was on a date, okay? He was a bit... unpredictable. I didn't feel right going home, so I asked him to drop me off here—just in case.”

Orion stares at her a beat longer, then shifts his attention back to the moment at hand.

“She was about to get into a black SUV,” Lisa continues, “And when I called out to her, his men had guns on me in a second. She stopped them before it got bad, but I clearly heard her telling them I was nobody, just some jealous woman.”

“CCTV,” Logan mutters, moving fast toward the security monitors.

I follow him and watch as he pulls up the footage. We cycle through angles until we catch them. Maisy. Viktor. His brothers. Moving toward the SUV like it's just any other day. I can barely recognize her beneath that mask she's wearing—detached, smiling like she belongs with them.

I feel my nails biting into my palms. “Fuck.”

Lisa crosses her arms. “Then, as they drove off,

she yelled through the window that she'll never leave Viktor." She glances at Orion. "Which was uncalled for, really."

Orion stares silently at the screen. Logan leans in closer, his jaw clenched so tight I think it might crack.

"Whatever she's doing, it's for a reason. But we don't want her to run out of time," Lisa says.

I shake my head, trying to steady my breathing. Logan flicks through more footage, zooming out to different angles of the street. Slavs. Everywhere. Leaning against cars, smoking, enjoying life. But I know better. I can see the outlines of guns beneath their coats, the way they shift, the readiness in their stances.

"They're ready for a fight," I say, the words tasting like iron. "All of them."

Logan nods, eyes glued to the screen. "If we start shooting down there, we'll lose. Too dense, too many innocent people around."

Lisa pipes up. "Think about it, Orion. Maisy would never do this, unless—"

"Unless what?" I cut in. "Unless she was playing us from the beginning? Unless this was always her plan?"

"Unless she had no choice," Lisa counters. "You need to get to her."

Logan's face hardens. "Not before our kids are safe. I don't care about that traitor. My children come first."

"Maisy is not a traitor," Lisa says firmly. "I know her. Something else is happening."

Orion stands up, agitation visible in every taut line of his body. "Once the kids land," he says, "we'll bring her home."

The coldness in his voice should shock me, but it doesn't. Part of me feels the same—rage and betrayal.

Logan checks his watch and turns to Orion. "Did your friend have any luck with their CCTV system?"

"I'll make sure he gets everything ready by tomorrow night," Orion says.

"We gotta figure out what game Viktor's playing." My fists clench at my sides. "And if Maisy's really part of his life, I'm gonna enjoy killing her."

The emptiness inside me transforms into purpose. Whether it's to save Maisy or kill her—I don't know yet. But either way, Viktor is a dead man walking. Has been for some time.

Orion catches my eye, and for a moment, I glimpse the same conflict there. The three of us, bound by blood, and by her. By what she gave us. By what we thought we had.

"Kai, Logan, get some rest. We haven't slept in days, and we'll need every ounce of strength if we're going to take that bastard down. We've got five, maybe six hours until the children land. Then it's a full day keeping them safe before we head out to DC in the evening."

ORION

"We've landed," Angelina says, her voice tight with tension. "Private airstrip. No one followed us."

Having just opened my eyes, relief floods through me.

"The kids?" Logan demands. He sounds as if he hasn't slept at all.

"Safe," Angelina responds.

"Stay alert," I interject. "Emilio should be there to pick you up."

Celina's voice comes through the speaker now. "Logan, what's happening with Maisy? The children keep asking for her."

Pain lances through my chest. The twins always ask for her first. Mama, then Daddy. Always in that order.

"We'll explain later," Logan says curtly. "Just keep them calm."

"Kai, hey, wake up." I nudge Kai a few times

before he responds by swinging his fist, luckily not towards me.

I'm already on my feet. My suit's wrinkled, the fabric worn, I don't think we've slept at all since Maisy disappeared.

"It's time." I cross the room to Logan's desk. "I'm letting my guy know, he must be through Ma Molly's security by end of day." I hunch over the laptop. I feel haunted, hollowed out. Like a man preparing to burn his own heart.

Maybe that's exactly what I am about to do.

LOGAN

The children arrived sleepy, wide-eyed, and clinging to the familiar hands of the three women who had kept them safe in Chicago—Angelina, Celina, and Sasha. It was early in the morning when they got here, and by the time they arrived, they were exhausted. Angelina carried Grace and Ava inside; Celina had Damien tucked against her shoulder. Luca clung to Sasha's hand like his life depended on it. Maxim held Mila's hand and lead her to her bedroom.

While the women, including Leila, brought the kids upstairs to get them cleaned and rested, I pulled up the camera feeds in the surveillance room. I reset all access codes and added a new layer of firewalls just in case. This wasn't just a safehouse anymore—it was the last line of defense.

Then we brought in six of our top men—trusted, lethal, and loyal. Two outside. Two stationed at the back door. The remaining two rotated inside. They knew the stakes. None of them asked questions.

We spent the rest of the time preparing for the night. Orion, Kai, and I mapped out Ma Molly's estate down to the last detail, studying patrol routes, security feeds, and guard shifts. We stocked up on gear, weapons, comms—anything we could use.

The plan was simple: breach the perimeter, scale the eastern wall where the security cameras have blind spots, take out the guards silently, and extract her before anyone knows we're there. No firefights, no mess—just precision. And if anything else is to happen, then the assignment is to kill that motherfucker.

With our plan airtight, we had five, maybe six hours until sunset. And we did want to spend them with the kids. They were awake by then, wide-eyed and full of questions.

When darkness finally fell, the house was locked down, fortified beyond standard military protocol. The children had been fed and tucked into bed by then, spread across three rooms upstairs. The women rotated watch duty, and I added silent motion alerts near the bedrooms—just in case.

~

Having driven for the last four hours, Emilio drops us outside Ma Molly's house. We move under the cover of night, our tactical black gear letting us blend into the darkness. Orion leads and Kai follows with me at the rear, my trusty blade always ready.

We reach the wall and throw grappling hooks that bite into the stone. One by one, we scale it, slipping over the top like shadows. I land silently, crouch low, and signal clear. We advance, avoiding every pool of light as we cut across manicured lawns.

Two guards round the corner. Orion takes out the first with a silenced pistol to the head. Kai handles the second, a blade sliding clean between ribs before the man even knows he's dead. We hide the bodies in the hedges and press on.

We find the side entrance to the house, pick the lock, and slip inside. The halls are quiet, save for footsteps in the distance—from guards, I assume. We move fast, clearing rooms, making our way through the house.

All of the rooms are open, and empty. With Ma Molly gone, I wouldn't be surprised if the house is already listed for sale.

Within the same hallway we come across a single locked door. We look at each other. I hope she's in here. Kai picks the lock, and within seconds, it clicks. We open the door just enough to slip inside.

I see her before she even registers we're here. Maisy. Huddled by the window, she turns, her face pale, eyes wide in terror.

"Maisy." Orion reaches her first. "We're getting you out."

She shakes her head, panic flaring in her eyes. "No. Y-You can't be here."

As per our plan, I check for any threats in the room. Clear. Kai secures the window, his body tense, ready.

"Are you hurt?" I finally ask, stepping closer and scanning her for injuries.

"You need to leave. Now," she says, louder than she should.

Kai edges closer. "Baby girl, we came for you."

She backs away, her eyes darting toward the door. Her hands tremble, but there's steel in her voice. "I'm not going anywhere with you. I'm staying with Viktor."

"You're staying with him, and he keeps you

locked in here?" Orion growls. "Why the fuck are you lying?"

"This is where I belong now," she says coldly, but the tremor in her voice is giving her away.

I step closer. "Sweetheart, we know you."

Her eyes flash. "You don't know anything. Viktor's giving me what you never could. Power. Position. Respect."

"You don't mean that," Kai snaps.

Her mask cracks, just for a moment. "He has my—" She stops herself, biting down on whatever truth she almost gave away. "I don't love any of you. I never did."

Orion's face shifts, and the darkness takes over. He lunges forward, his hand snapping around her throat, pinning her to the wall. Her head hits it hard and I hear her gasp. Her nails claw at his wrist, drawing blood, but his grip doesn't loosen.

"Orion!" I grab him and yank him back.

Kai shoves himself between them, his back to Maisy, his voice like ice. "Touch her again and I'll break your hands."

Maisy crumples, coughing, dragging in air. I crouch beside her, one hand steady on her shoulder. "Take it easy."

Orion's eyes are still wild, but Kai keeps him back.

"Viktor will know you were here," Maisy gasps. "Go! You must—"

"Let him come," Kai snarls.

She shakes her head, desperation in her eyes. "You don't understand. He has my babies. Our babies."

The words gut me. The air leaves the room.

I take her arm. "No, Maisy. We have them. They're safe."

"W-What?" she asks, barely audible.

"They're at our house," Kai says, his voice gentler now. "They got back from Chicago, and they're with Sasha, Leila, Angelina, and Celina."

She stares, her mind spinning. "Viktor said—"

"He lied," Kai cuts in.

I see her calculating, the fear shifting, but not gone. "If he finds out—"

"He won't," I assure her. "We're ending this tonight."

She shakes her head. "No. The Council meeting's nine days from now. Every crime family in America will be there. If we wait…"

I check my watch. "Four minutes before the patrol circles back."

"I have to stay," she says firmly. "Viktor must believe I'm loyal. It's the only way."

Kai steps closer. "Not happening. We're not leaving you."

"I can handle Viktor," she insists.

"Like you've handled everything else?" Orion snaps. "I nearly killed you just now."

"Maisy," I urge, "we don't have time."

"The children—" she starts.

"Are safe," Kai says, steady. "And they need their mother."

"If I walk out, Viktor will hunt us all down."

"You won't have to walk," Orion says, and nods to me.

I pull out the syringe and administer the ketamine. She tries to protest, but it's too late. Her limbs go heavy. She attempts to speak but her words are slurred.

Kai catches her as she slumps, lifting her easily.

"We've got you," I murmur, brushing her hair from her forehead and checking her vitals.

Orion stands over us, his rage giving way to concern.

We move. Silent. Swift. The night closes in behind us as we take her home.

ORION

I stare at my knuckles—they're raw and reddened. These hands nearly choked the life out of Maisy. What kind of monster am I?

Viktor's manipulations don't absolve me. I should have known better, should have trusted her. Maisy would never betray our children. What's bothering me is that I never thought I'd have such a visceral reaction to her rejection of us. Even if there was doubt, I should never have put my hands on her. Never.

Dawn light filters through the windows, while outside, armed men, double the usual number, move along the property's edge. We've left nothing to chance—not anymore. This house holds everything that's precious to us, and I would burn the world down before letting danger cross this threshold.

Emilio drove through the night, determined to get us home before dawn. He knew the kids would be up early. He wanted us here when they opened their eyes.

For fuck's sake, had I killed her, what would have been my excuse? Would I have told them that I let my rage override my judgment? That I failed the one person who trusted me to protect her?

Kai and Logan went to our bedroom to change, but I haven't moved from this place.

Inside Maisy's room, I hear rustling. After five

hours of sleeping in the car, she's awake. I should go to her, but anger still roots me to the spot. I'm not angry at her, but at myself. She shouldn't have been so realistic. Right now, I hate her as much as I desperately love her.

Footsteps patter down the hall—small ones, quick and eager. The twins. And then the rest of them. They rush past me without a glance, pushing open the door to Maisy's room. They played with us yesterday. It's their mother they are after now.

"Mommy!" Their voices blend into a joyful duet.

More footsteps follow—heavier this time. Logan rounds the corner. "You look like shit," he says to me, voice low enough that the kids won't hear.

I don't respond. Everyone's grating on my nerves right now. There's nothing I could say to excuse my actions, and yet, I believe she bears just as much blame as I do.

Kai appears behind him. "Come in, apologize, and it'll be over."

My jaw clenches so tight my teeth might break. The thought of surrendering when she's the one who— no. Apologize? The bitter taste of near-betrayal floods my mouth. Something wounded inside me refuses to bend.

"I've taken you for many things, but never a coward," Kai comments, brushing past me to enter the room.

Logan follows him, but not before dropping a hand on my shoulder. The touch feels like forgiveness I don't deserve.

I edge closer to the doorway, keeping out of sight but close enough to hear.

One of the twins climbs onto the bed. "Mom! We missed you!"

"Careful," Angelina warns, appearing from somewhere inside the room. "Your mommy needs rest."

"I missed you too." Maisy's voice is hoarse, damaged. Because of me. "Come here, all of you."

I hear the bed creak as more children pile on. My chest constricts. This is what I almost destroyed—this perfect, chaotic family.

"We were scared on the airplane," one of the kids says, "but Sasha told us it's tahbulance."

"I know, sweetheart." Maisy's voice cracks. "But I'm sure you were brave." There's a pause. "Thank you so much for keeping my babies safe." Her words are directed at Angelina and Celina.

"Always," Celina responds. "Are you feeling okay? Kai told us what Orion did."

Here it comes—her hatred, her disgust. All deserved.

"Yeah, forget it," Maisy says, dismissing her own pain like it's nothing. "I deserved that for not listening to him."

"Well, it was stupid of him to think you'd betray your kids," Angelina says with her characteristic bluntness. "I mean, come on. What planet does he live on?"

Kai clears his throat. "Maisy was extremely believable, and...strangely cold. I don't know." I can picture him shrugging. He's trying to stand up for me, for us.

"She had to be," Celina replies. "Would you have half-assed it if you were in her shoes?"

"You're probably right," Kai concedes.

"How were we supposed to know?" Logan shoots back defensively.

"Isn't Orion coming?" Maisy's request carries out into the hall. Asking for me.

I'm not ready to be faced with the bruises I left on her throat, but I'm no coward either. "Viktor made me hurt the one thing that I live for," I growl to the empty hallway, "and he'll pay for that."

I turn and push the door fully open.

Why is my heart pounding against my ribs like it's trying to escape? Maybe it already knows it doesn't belong to me anymore. It's hers—has been since the moment she crashed into my life.

The room falls silent when I step inside. Six pairs of children's eyes turn to me, their expressions ranging from curiosity to wariness. Logan and Kai exchange a look I can't decipher. Angelina and Celina move subtly, positioning themselves between me and Maisy—ready to defend her from me.

"Daddy!!" Mila exclaims, and opens her arms.

But it's Maisy's gaze that pins me in place. The bruising around her throat is visible, even in the dim morning light.

"Could everyone give us a minute?" I ask. I pick up Mila, kiss her cheek, and pass her on to Celina.

"It's breakfast time, gang," Kai says, gathering up the twins. Logan helps herd the rest of the children.

As they file past me, Logan squeezes my shoulder again. A reminder that I'm not alone, even when I deserve to be.

Maisy's lying in bed, wearing her robe.

"I did what I had to do to protect our children," I say, and sit next to her on the bed.

"I did the same thing," she responds.

"And I'd do it again if I thought you were working against us." It's the truth.

Her eyes narrow. "Is that supposed to scare me?"

"No," I say evenly. "It's just the truth."

She takes a breath, then reaches for my hands. "Me too."

I squeeze her hands and nod.

"So we're good?" she asks quietly.

I pinch her chin and pull her face closer to me so

I can look deep into her eyes. "Seeing you with someone else was heart-wrenching. And I don't say that lightly. I never imagined it was possible to feel so much pain. You, Maisy, you're my weakness. Your power over me terrifies me, now more than ever. And I don't think I can handle it."

"It's okay to be vulnerable, Orion." She strokes my face, her voice and her touch soothing my soul. "I made my choice to protect our family. You made the same choice. And both of us ended up with nightmares." She sighs. "The images of you three still flash through my mind. My curse, my photographic memory, won't let me forget a single detail of what I've done. Your face when I took Viktor's side. The shock in Logan's eyes. Kai's anger as he lunged at us, only to be knocked almost unconscious." Her voice drops, barely above a whisper. "I've spent my life calculating risks, manipulating situations, using my head to stay one step ahead. But this wasn't a calculation. This was surrender." She looks at me and hesitates as her eyes gloss over. "...There was a moment when I really thought I couldn't do it. When everything inside me screamed at me to give up—that there was no hope left. But then, you asked me on the phone if I remembered what I told you when the twins were born. I will never be able to love you as much as I will love my babies. That moment, Orion, something shifted inside me. And I knew—I would survive. I would win. Not because I wasn't afraid. But because giving up stopped being an option. I had to think of my babies. As I said to you back then."

I take her hand again and kiss it. "That asshole will pay for what he's done."

"Not yet." Her fingers tighten around mine. "I have a plan." She tugs me closer until I'm lying beside her, and she places her head on my chest. "And you won't like it one little bit."

I press a kiss to her head. "I'm sure I won't. But seeing you out there, alone, more powerful than all of us, even under duress, I don't doubt you for one moment."

She tilts her face up and smiles. "Mess with my family, you mess with me."

I trace the edge of her jaw, checking what I've done, being careful to avoid the bruising. "Never again, Maisy. I swear it on my life."

"Good." She settles against me, her breathing evening out. "Because if you ever try it again, I'll kill you myself." She titters.

We lie there in silence as the household slowly comes to life around us. Outside the door, I hear the children's chatter, the rumble of Logan's voice as he prepares breakfast, and Celina and Angelina's laughter as they entertain our kids.

CHAPTER 14

LOGAN

The sound of children's laughter echoes through our home, a small miracle after the hell we've all been through. I lean against the doorframe of the living room, watching Maisy on the floor with the kids. All six of them—I still marvel at how she manages them all.

"Logan, you just gonna stand there or help me with these tiny monsters?" Maisy calls out as Grace climbs onto her back.

"Just appreciating the view." I smile. Something is different about her. The way she holds herself, maybe. More confident? No, that isn't it. But something has shifted.

Our moment is interrupted by the doorbell.

Again. The third time in an hour.

"I'll get it," Kai announces, striding past me. When he opens the door, I see Georgina.

"She here?" Georgina's not bothering with pleasantries. Especially after the way we treated her.

"Yes, I'm here." Maisy steps forward, gently passing Grace into my arms. "They're all waiting in the dining room," she adds, with a subtle nod toward the hallway.

Our dining room has turned into some kind of council for women. Celina, Lisa, Angelina, and Sasha are already there, hunched over coffee cups, and more women are expected, I'm told. Their voices are a steady hum of conversation that drops suspiciously when I enter. They've all been trying to find out what Maisy went through with that asshole.

"That's not gossip," Maisy insisted earlier when I raised an eyebrow at their huddled conversations. "It's strategic information sharing."

Later, when the kids are settled with their movies and toys, and of course, with Sasha by their side, we finally notice that Maisy's friends have left.

Orion corners Maisy in the kitchen. I follow, with Kai close behind. We need answers.

"Maisy," Orion begins, "it's been a few days now. It's time we talk about what happened."

Maisy looks between the three of us. She picks

up a mug of coffee and takes a sip. Her onyx eyes reveal nothing. Then, out of the blue, she takes us by surprise.

"Tell me, if we had gotten married by now, would we have had this problem?"

I'm stunned, and unsure what to say. We all glance at each other before Orion takes the lead.

"No, we wouldn't have had this problem. Because if we'd married you, your share of New York would've belonged to us."

Maisy raises her eyebrows. "You?"

"Well, when I say us, I mean you too—because then you'd officially be part of the family. Don't forget, we already run New York, but if we were married, it would be in an official capacity," Orion explains.

"So for now, you're running it unofficially?" she asks. I'm not sure if she's trying to grasp the situation or just reaffirming information she already has.

"Yes. Because you're not the head of the mafia like your father was. You're our woman now, so we took control of it. But as we've learned, anyone can challenge that control—since it's not official."

"So basically, this was all your fault," she concludes.

"Yes," Orion says softly. "And I'm sorry for that. We struggled to tell you. We didn't want you to think we only wanted to marry you for your stake. And while we hesitated...time just kept slipping by."

"Fools," she says, enunciating it. "You men are fools."

Kai nods. "Agreed."

"It's too late now," she snaps, irritation slipping into her voice. "You wanted to talk about what happened, right?"

"Correct," Orion says, shifting his stance. She's clearly caught all of us off guard with her questions.

"Viktor took you," I say, playing with the blade in my pocket. The feel of it reminds me of who it is for.

"Did he try something?" Kai demands. "Because if he touched you—"

Maisy cuts him off. "He didn't."

She leans against the counter, looking at us not like someone who needs protecting, or saving, but like an equal. It throws me. I really expected tears, trauma—especially after what happened last time she was kidnapped, and what she went through. What both of us went through back then. Instead, she's talking clinically about her own kidnapping.

"Georgina found me a condo I could stay in, but they tracked my cell just before I switched it off. And then found me hiding under the bed," she explains, her voice steady despite the memory. "Viktor and his three brothers. They dragged me out by my ankles while I screamed."

Something primal twists in my gut. With my

hand in my pocket, my fingers curl so hard around the handle of the blade I feel my knuckles might split. The image of Maisy being dragged burns itself into my brain.

Orion's voice drops an octave. "Those fuckers."

"Then I was hit on the head with something, and—"

"Fuck," Kai swears, but all I can think about is concussion. Brain swelling. Hemorrhage. The possibilities flash through my mind and make my blood run cold.

"I woke up two days later, in a basement, my wrists and my ankles tied to a bedframe, with Viktor and his men standing over me." Maisy narrows her eyes. "He was gloating. Asshole. He said he couldn't wait to kill me. He said eliminating me was the only way he'd become head of the Slavs."

The veins in Kai's neck are visible as he slams his fist hard on the counter. "I'm gonna paint the walls with his blood!"

"Get in line, Kai," Maisy replies, her calmness unsettling me. "I made him think that, since I'm a Slav, I could help him rule."

"And that worked?" Orion asks, leaning forward.

"Viktor's arrogant." A sneer plays on her lips. "He thinks he's the smartest person in any room."

I cross my arms. "What are you saying?"

"I had to do what I had to do, because the lives of

my children were at stake. I was threatened and trapped. But now?" Her voice has drops to a deadly whisper. "He's gonna find out that nobody gets to threaten my children and live."

She sets down her mug and slides past Kai and me with predatory grace, stalking toward the living room.

"What the fuck?" I mutter, making sure only Orion and Kai hear me.

Orion's eyes meet mine, then shift to Kai. Before we can say anything, Orion's cell rings.

"Oh, that must be Uncle Colletti and Uncle Leo," Maisy says, turning back to us. She has that look—the one that means her brain is ten steps ahead. "They'll want to apologize."

"For what?" Kai asks.

"For doubting me," she says, a hint of satisfaction in her voice. "When I showed up at the penthouse with Viktor, they were gloating, if you didn't notice."

I remember the day with sickening clarity—Maisy walking in, on someone else's arm. The doubt that clouded my own judgment.

"You knew they never trusted you," Orion states.

Kai's eyebrows shoot up. "Damn."

"I had enough of their negativity," she rejoins us. "And now that they've seen I was loyal the entire time..."

Orion answers his cell, putting it on speaker. "Carte."

"Hey, Orion. Is Maisy there?" Uncle Leo's gruff voice fills the kitchen, sounding uncharacteristically hesitant.

"I'm here," she says calmly.

"Listen," he begins awkwardly, "we were wrong about you."

Uncle Colletti's voice joins in. "We misjudged you. Shouldn't have been so quick to believe you'd turned."

I watch a small, victorious smile play at the corners of Maisy's lips.

"No harm done," she says, though we all know that's not entirely true. "I showed Viktor exactly what he needed to see—that not everyone here supports me. A division he could exploit."

Silence hangs on the line as the realization dawns on both men. They've been played, but for a purpose bigger than their pride.

"Smart," Uncle Leo admits finally. "Risky as hell, but smart."

"Mm-hmm." Now she's cocky.

"Well, anyway. Goodbye," Uncle Colletti says, and the line goes dead.

Kai looks at Maisy with something between admiration and horror. "Damn, baby girl."

"Kai, I think I was clear. Viktor, and everyone else he brought with him, is not getting out of this alive."

"Easy now, we don't want you getting yourself kidnapped again," I warn. "And please, for the sake of our kids, don't do anything stupid."

Orion doesn't say anything for a moment. He remains silent, his dark eyes tracking Maisy's every movement. His face reveals nothing, so I can't tell if he's buying into her performance or dismissing it. He simply observes, taking in every micro-expression, every gesture. Orion isn't being taken in by clever Maisy—he's measuring her.

"Maisy," he finally says, his brows knitted, "I haven't seen you like this before. This intensity...this focus. There's rage inside you, but you've contained it like a weapon. It's the control that's unsettling. You're not just angry—you're methodical about it. Calculated. It's like watching a predator decide exactly when and how to strike."

Maisy just shrugs and heads to the living room.

She sinks onto the sofa and kicks her feet up on the coffee table. I follow and sit next to her.

"Level with me," I say quietly, "are you really okay?"

She looks at me and for just a moment, I see a flicker of vulnerability in the depths of her eyes—a glimpse of the fear she's hidden from everyone else.

"I was terrified," she whispers. "But I couldn't show it. Not to him. Not to anyone."

I press my forehead against hers. "You don't have to be strong all the time. Not with us."

"Yes, I do." Her voice is firm again. "Six children depend on me. Three mafia families think of me as their woman. And as such, I can't afford weakness."

I kiss her then, gently. "Being human isn't weakness, sweetheart."

She pulls back, that new determination hardening her features. "You're wrong, Logan. In our world, it's the most dangerous thing to be." Her eyes meet mine. "Humanity is what they target first. They see it, they exploit it, they destroy it. Well, I'm calling the shots now. And I bet you, Viktor is not going to like that one little bit."

CHAPTER 15

ORION

I lean against my desk, watching the security detail through the window of my office. Six men patrol the perimeter of the property, and another four guard the front door. All are heavily armed.

The sun has just begun to set, and in the fading light, I see my own reflection in the glass. Beyond my dark eyes, I see the world I've built. The world I'd kill to protect.

I close my eyes, Maisy's words from earlier today, reminding us that the clock is ticking, still ring in my ears.

"In seven days' time, Viktor will make his move, he'll become the head of the Slavs at the Council

Meeting."

"Fuck," I mutter to myself, running a hand through my hair.

I turn away from the window and pace the length of my office. The weight of my Colt pressing against my ribs is the only thing that comforts me at this moment.

I think about that first time Viktor came to our penthouse, bold as brass, uninvited—we should have put a bullet between his eyes. We should have ended the threat before it began.

The knock at my office door is so faint I almost miss it. I don't need to turn to know who it is—only one person in this house knocks that softly.

"Come in, darling," I call out, my voice automatically softening.

But the door remains closed. I frown, crossing the room in three long strides and pulling it open myself.

The hallway is empty.

My hand instinctively moves toward my holster before I catch myself. Paranoia. This house is secure—I designed the security system myself. No one gets in or out without my knowledge.

I close the door again, pressing my forehead against the cool wood, remembering Maisy's words.

"Viktor Mrozovski has petitioned for a quarter of New York," she said, her voice steady despite the gravity of the situation. "He's gone through the proper channels. The Council has agreed to hear his case. But that was when they had me."

The memory of Kai's reaction pulls my lips into a grim smile. He exploded exactly as I'd expect—all rage and impulse, slamming his fist on the table hard enough to rattle our glasses.

"We should've killed that fucker when we had the chance!" he shouted, eyes blazing. "When he walked into our fucking home like he owned the place! Now he's got the Council's ear?!"

Logan remained silent, but his eyes met mine across the table, and I knew we were thinking the same thing.

Kai was right.

We'd had our chance, and we'd missed it. That day at the penthouse, we could have ended it then. Three shots. Three bullets. Problem solved.

But we'd played politics instead of pulling triggers. And now Viktor is making his play through legitimate channels. The kind of move that even men like us can't simply ignore without consequences.

I move back to the window, watching as the security lights automatically switch on around the perimeter of our estate. Our house is fortified better than most military installations, a sanctuary, one I've built for our family.

A memory of Viktor comes to me, and how he looked at her. I should have killed him for that look alone.

After Maisy delivered the news about the Council meeting, we strategized for hours. I outlined our legal options. Kai pushed for immediate action—a pre-emptive strike to eliminate the threat before the meeting could take place. Maisy listened to all of us, her brilliant mind working through possibilities and probabilities with that eerie calculation that still unnerves me sometimes.

The sound of the door opening behind me pulls me from my thoughts. I don't turn, but I feel her presence—the subtle shift in the air that always accompanies Maisy when she enters a room.

"I stopped by earlier, but Mia called me in the last moment," she says, her voice soft but clear. "The children are finally in bed. And Mia wanted you to know she finished the book you gave her."

I nod, still facing the window. "Smart girl."

"So's her uncle."

I can hear the smile in her voice, and despite everything, I feel the corners of my mouth lift in response. I turn to face her then, drinking in the sight of her—dark curls falling loose around her shoulders, onyx eyes that miss nothing, the curve of her lips that I know better than my own name.

"What are you thinking?" she asks, crossing the room to stand beside me at the window.

"That Kai was right," I admit. "We should've killed Viktor when we had the chance."

Her hand finds mine, our fingers intertwining naturally. "Yes," she agrees simply.

"The Council meeting changes everything," I continue. "Viktor's not just some upstart trying to muscle in anymore. He's playing by the old rules."

"Rules you ought to respect," she notes, her thumb tracing circles on the back of my hand.

I nod. I'm a lawyer by training, a criminal by birth. The duality has always served me well—it's allowed me to navigate both worlds with equal skill. I understand the importance of institutions like the Council, even as I subvert them for my own purposes.

"If we move against him now, before the Council hearing, we risk alienating the other families," I say, thinking aloud. "But if we wait..."

"If we wait, he gains legitimacy," Maisy finishes for me. "And legitimacy means power."

"Exactly." I squeeze her hand gently. "And he's already too powerful for my liking."

"The meeting's in a week," she says. "We need to find something concrete on him before then. Something the Council can't ignore."

"You think there's dirt?"

"There's always something," she replies with certainty. "No one's record is clean. Especially not a man like Viktor."

I release her hand and move to my desk, sit down, and unlock the bottom drawer. From it, I withdraw a thick file—everything Logan, Kai, and I have compiled on Viktor since his arrival in the city.

"Logan and I have been through this a dozen times," I say, dropping it on the desk with a thud. "There's nothing we can use that wouldn't implicate us as well."

Maisy approaches the desk, placing her palm flat on its surface as she leans over the file. "Let me try. A fresh perspective."

I watch her as she goes through it, her eyes moving rapidly over the pages, absorbing every detail. Her photographic memory is more than just a party trick—it's a weapon in its own right. She'll remember every word, every number, every connection.

"There's something here," she murmurs, prodding at a page halfway through the file. "A pattern."

I lean in, close enough to catch the scent of her perfume. "What do you see?"

"His shipments from North Macedonia," she says, flipping back and forth between pages. "The manifests don't match. Look—the weight differences are inconsistent. Small enough to go unnoticed individually, but when you add them up…”

I follow her logic. “He’s smuggling.”

“Yes, but not in the way you think.” Her finger traces a column of numbers. “These aren’t drugs or weapons. The weight and frequency suggest something else.” She looks up at me, horror gleaming in her eyes. “People, Orion. He’s trafficking people.”

Human trafficking is the one line none of the established families would cross. Even in our world, there are boundaries. Rules. And this is the one that, if broken, would turn every family against him.

My mind is already racing ahead. “Can we prove it?”

Maisy shakes her head. “We don’t have time for that.”

I watch her continue to pore over the documents. “If you’re right about this, the Council won’t just reject his petition, they’ll sanction a hit,” I tell her.

She looks up at me, those dark eyes unflinching. “I know.”

“And if you’re wrong…”

“I’m not wrong,” she says, with absolute certainty.

I reach out, tucking a strand of hair behind her ear, my fingers lingering against her cheek. “This is why I love you, darling.”

A small smile curves her lips. “Because I can find

patterns in shipping manifests?"

"Because nothing escapes you," I correct as she comes over to my side of the desk. "Not even the things Viktor Mrozovski thinks he's hidden."

I pull her gently into my lap, my arms circling her waist as she settles against me. Her fingers trace the edge of my tattoo above my collar, and she leans in and presses her lips chastely to mine. I expect that to be it, but she rakes her fingers through my hair and intensifies the kiss. Her tongue weaves passionately with mine; it almost feels odd, especially from her, because she wouldn't be into topping from the bottom, I'm sure.

"Would you let me fuck you?" she whispers against my lips.

I chuckle. This confident Maisy, who thinks she can fuck me, has a lot to learn.

"Absolutely..." I nip her lower lip. "...not. But you can ride my cock if you want. I won't stop you." I nip her jaw and continue down her neck as I unbutton her shirt. "Do you know why I won't stop you?"

She grins, and bares her breasts from her bra cups the moment I'm done unbuttoning, waiting on me to suck them and play with them.

"Why?" she breathes.

"Because you're my whore," I mumble into her skin, "and you'll do what I tell you to."

Her hips have begun gyrating softly over my

cock and as I play with her breasts, her movements grow more insistent.

"My personal slut." I bite and pull at her nipple. "To share as I please." I knead her other breast and rub the nipple. "To fuck when I want." I unbutton her jeans and slide my hand down inside her panties. "To use as a cum bucket."

"Orion..." Maisy moans.

I run my fingers between her folds. Her wet cunt is ready for me. She tries to stroke my cock over my pants, but I put my hand over hers, squeeze it, then take it away and thread our fingers together. I look at the darkness in her eyes, the real her that craves to be seen, before I devour her mouth, weaving my tongue with hers.

I stand up, taking her with me. "And right this very moment, your purpose is just that."

I spin her around and bend her over my desk. In one move, I pull down her jeans and panties, revealing her sweet, juicy ass.

"Yeees..." I stroke her butt cheeks. "This is good, very good, Maisy," I mutter, nearly losing my mind with the need I have for her.

I slide my index and middle fingers inside and coat them in her juice, hearing her whine as I take them out and swirl the arousal over her nub. The second time, I jerk my fingers deeper, to the knuckle, and do this a few times before she bucks and raises her hips into my fingers. I collect her arousal on my way out and rub it over her swollen clit.

"You like this, don't you, whore?"

"Y-Yes," she moans as I continue sliding my fingers inside her and rubbing her nub. I repeat the motion, over and over, until she throws her head back. "Orion!" she cries.

A rush of cum dribbles out of her cunt and her hips jerk up into my hand as she rides the waves of her orgasm. I hurriedly unbutton my jeans with my free hand. The moment my cock is out, I fist it and pump a few times, the precum running down over my piercing. I withdraw my soaked fingers from inside her and bring them to my lips.

"Oh, fuck! Why do you taste so divine?" I wasn't planning on eating her as my cock craves her as much as my tongue, but tasting her now, I know my cock will have to wait. I kneel down behind her, spread open her butt cheeks and press the flat of my tongue against her cunt, now soaked with arousal. My tongue slides from her sweet nub up to her asshole, stirring incomprehensible sounds from her as she helps me by spreading her legs just a little bit further.

I push my tongue inside her cunt, lapping up everything she has. I hold her butt cheeks firmly open, keeping her in place, and she bucks downward against my mouth, jolting and moaning as I continue to devour her swollen nub.

"There, just there!" She jerks her hips again, right into my tongue as I lap up her juices. My tongue swirls over her nub, and I suck on that little fucker while pushing two fingers inside. Her thighs begin to tremble and she fully unravels into a long moan.

"Orion!" she whimpers.

I get to my feet before she's down from her heaven and with my cock hard as steel, I begin to enter her ass, my piercing breaching her slowly. She realizes she's going to stay high for a while, and hums in approval. I push again, and again; each time she allows me to go deeper, gushing so much arousal that my balls are soaked as I stretch her out. Her ass is going to be the death of me. She's taking me inch by inch, and I'm nearly halfway in when her long, whining moans encourage me to slide the rest of my cock in until I'm balls-deep.

"There you go. Your ass is mine now!"

She looks back at me over her shoulder, her pupils dilated, her fingers curled around the edge of the desk, holding on for leverage as I claw at her hips and start pumping her deep, hard, grunting with each thrust.

She reaches between her legs, rubbing herself as I slam into her, whining like she's flying up to cloud nine, right where I am.

"You want my cum, whore?"

"Y-Yes," she begs.

"Hmm?" I grunt.

"Yes, please," she huffs between thrusts.

I'm so close to orgasming. "Why?"

"B-Because I'm y-your cum bucket," she whimpers. She's starting to come undone again. Her whole body's vibrating.

"Correct!" Electrifying, staccato moans fall from her lips and I increase the pace; her back arches and her head falls back. "Never forget that!"

One last thrust and I still, feeling my cock spurting cum inside her cunt. Halfway through my release, I pull out and pump a few more ropes over the crack of her ass, watching it dribble down into her gaping entrance.

Still clawing at her hips, I growl, long and loud. "Fuck! Maisy, you're my whore forever!"

CHAPTER 16

ORION

"You're up early." Logan enters the room and stops beside me.

I don't look up, staying to watch as our security disperse to their assigned positions around the perimeter. "So are you."

"That's twenty-four men on rotation now," he observes. "Plus the usual household security."

"It's not enough," I reply, finally turning to face him.

Logan nods.

"We got Maisy out from under Viktor's nose," I add. "He won't forgive that humiliation."

"True. But don't forget, he's petitioned the

Council," Logan reminds me. "He has to play by the rules."

"For now," I counter. "Although, something tells me that he doesn't lose gracefully."

Logan's jaw tightens. We all know what Viktor intended for Maisy—the thought alone makes my hands curl into fists.

The sound of heavy boots in the hallway announces Kai's arrival before he appears in the doorway, his blond hair pulled back in a messy knot. Unlike Logan and me, he makes no pretense of refinement. The leather jacket, the boots, the ring that doubles as a weapon—Kai wears his violence openly, a warning to anyone who might cross him.

"That army outside is the best kind of good morning. When are we attacking?" he demands.

"We need to talk," I say, gesturing for him to close the door.

Kai's eyes narrow, but he complies, shutting the door with a soft click that somehow feels more ominous than if he'd slammed it. "Is this about Viktor?" he asks, moving to stand beside Logan.

"It's about Maisy," I say. Nothing unites us more quickly than concern for her. "But yes, it involves Viktor."

I move to my desk. "In six days, the Council will meet, but we know Viktor won't wait for its decision if he sees an opportunity for revenge." I look at them both. "Which is why we need to take precautions." I straighten, my decision already made. "I think you'll all agree with me when I say that Maisy shouldn't leave this house until after the Council meeting."

We all understand what this entails. Maisy, with her fierce independence and hatred of confinement, will not take this well.

"She won't like it," Logan says, voicing what we're all thinking.

"I don't give a damn if she likes it or not," I reply. "I care that she's alive. Don't you?"

"You're right. Viktor would kill her on sight if he got the chance," Kai agrees.

"Not just kill her," Logan adds quietly. "He'd make an example of her. To send a message to anyone who might consider defying him in the future."

We've all seen Viktor's handiwork before—what he's capable of. The thought of Maisy in his hands again makes my blood run cold.

"So we're agreed?" I ask, looking from one to the other. "Maisy stays inside, under protection, until the Council meeting is resolved."

Logan nods, his expression grim. "The children should stay in as well."

"I've already arranged for additional household help," I say. "Angelina and Celina will come here—

they're vetted and loyal—but no one else enters without explicit clearance from one of us."

The door opens suddenly, without a knock, and there she is—as if conjured up by our conversation.

Maisy stands in the doorway, her dark hair framing a face that would look innocent if not for the knowing gleam in her eyes. She's in her night slip, but she commands the room's attention instantly.

"Explicit clearance?" she asks, her gaze moving between the three of us.

None of us speaks. Even with our combined power, our combined ruthlessness, telling Maisy what to do is not something any of us approach lightly.

"Well?" she prompts, stepping fully into the room and closing the door behind her. "What secret are my three overprotective mafia heads keeping now?"

I exchange glances with Logan and Kai, a silent communication passing between us. This is my call to make, my edict to deliver.

"Viktor's a sore loser," I say, watching her reaction carefully. "We have reason to believe that he'll come after you."

Maisy's expression doesn't change. "I'm aware of that."

"Then you're also aware of the danger," I continue. "Viktor won't wait for the Council's ruling if he sees an opportunity for revenge."

"He's predictable that way," she agrees, coming to stand on the other side of the desk from me. "So what's the plan you three have devised without consulting me?"

There it is: the edge in her voice that warns us that Maisy hates being controlled, hates decisions being made about her life without her input. And here I am, about to confirm I'm doing just that.

"You're not leaving the house until after the Council meeting," I tell her, keeping my voice firm. "The children will stay in as well. Angelina and Celina can come to help, but no one else enters without our approval."

Maisy's dark eyes meet mine, unflinching. "So I'm a prisoner again. How convenient."

"Not a prisoner," Kai interjects, stepping forward. "Protected, baby girl. There's a difference."

"Is there?" she asks, her gaze shifting to him. "Because from where I'm standing, being told I can't leave my home feels remarkably like captivity."

Logan moves closer, like he's hoping to soothe her. "It's only for a few days, Maisy. Just until we can ensure Viktor doesn't have the Council's backing."

"And if the Council rules in his favor?" she challenges. "What then? Do I stay locked away indefinitely?"

"The Council won't rule in his favor," I say, with

more confidence than I feel. "Not once we tell them of his operations."

Maisy turns back to me, her expression cool. "You seem very certain of that, Orion. Almost as if you've forgotten how many of the Council members could be in Viktor's pocket already."

"Not enough to override a formal denouncement," I counter. "Not if we prove he's broken the most sacred rule."

"What about the evidence?" she asks.

"Your shipping manifest analysis was the key. Logan's contacts at the port confirmed unusual medical supply requests corresponding with the shipment arrivals. We're building a case."

"A case that would be stronger if I could follow up with my sources in person," she points out, crossing her arms over her chest.

"A case that means nothing if you're dead," Kai snaps, his patience evidently wearing thin.

Maisy's eyes flash. "I survived in this world long before I had three mafia lords hovering over me, Kai. I've come a long way from that delicate flower that needed constant protection."

"No one thinks you're delicate," Logan says carefully, "but Viktor's different. He's obsessed. And obsession makes men dangerous."

"Don't I know it," she murmurs, her gaze sliding

meaningfully to me.

I feel the subtle jab, but don't rise to it. "If we don't count today, that's five days, Maisy. All we're asking is five days of caution."

She studies me for a long moment. "Fine," she finally says. "Five days. But I have conditions."

"Name them."

"I want full access to all intelligence coming in about Viktor's operations. No filtering, no editing to 'protect' me." She holds up a hand as Kai begins to protest. "I can't help build the case against him if I don't have all the information."

"Done," I agree.

"Second, I want to have calls with my contacts. If I can't meet them in person, I need to maintain those relationships remotely."

Logan frowns. "Calls can be intercepted—"

She cuts him off. "Then make them secure. Figure it out."

I nod slowly. "We can arrange secure communications. What else?"

Maisy's expression softens slightly. "The children need routine. Structure. Being confined will be hard enough without them feeling like prisoners too. I want to maintain as much normalcy as possible."

"Of course," I agree. "Their tutors will continue lessons remotely."

Maisy's shoulders relax fractionally. "Last condition. When this is over—when the Council has given its ruling—no matter the outcome, this protection detail ends. I won't live in a gilded cage, not even one built by the men I love."

Love is a dangerous concept in our world, a vulnerability none of us can afford. And yet here we are, four people who have built an empire on that very foundation.

"Agreed," I say after a moment. "But if Viktor remains a threat—"

"Then we deal with it together," she interrupts. "As equals. Not with you three making decisions about my life without me."

Kai steps to her side, slipping an arm around her shoulders. "You're always our equal, baby girl—even if you might need a little more protecting sometimes. But hey, that's what we're here for."

A small smile tugs at her lips despite her obvious irritation. "Nice try, but flattery's not getting you out of the doghouse, Kai."

"Worth a try," he grins, pressing a kiss to her temple.

Logan interjects, his expression serious. "I'll start making arrangements for your calls. Secure channels, untraceable."

"I'll brief the security team," I add. "And speak

with Angelina and Celina about their hours here."

Maisy looks between the three of us again, her dark eyes softening. "You know I understand the necessity, right? I just hate feeling trapped."

"It's not forever," I promise, moving around the desk to stand before her. "Just long enough to ensure Viktor can't hurt you or the children."

She nods, reaching up to straighten my tie, a casual yet intimate gesture. "Five days," she agrees. "And then we end this."

The determination in her voice reminds me why all three of us—hardened criminals, ruthless killers, men who command empires built on violence and fear— would move heaven and earth for this woman. It isn't just love. It's respect. Admiration.

"Deal," I say, taking her hand and pressing a kiss to her knuckles. "Five days of caution, and then we strike."

Her smile is slow, dangerous, beautiful. "I already have some ideas about that part."

CHAPTER 17

DAY 1

MAISY

I never wanted power. Being born a Slavinovich has cursed both my life and my sister's. People like Milan, and everyone else, exploited it. Trauma, tragedy, and turmoil, that's what power is in my world. That's the reason I chose to live a quiet life with my men and my children. And up until now, my life with my family has made me happy. Even setting up the club felt good because I was contributing in a subtle, indirect way.

But this man, Viktor, he's forcing me down a one-way street. In a direction I've been avoiding for quite some time. Viktor thinks he can take what's mine. What was laid to rest thanks to the Cartes, Vitalis, and Delgados. He thinks he can kill me, and my children too—and somewhere in between, hurt my men. The thought brings a bitter smile to my face. He has no idea what I'm capable of. I wouldn't necessarily have this bravado if it was only my life at stake. But going after my children, and my men? My body comes alive with the need for retaliation—it feels as if a demon inside me just woke up. Like that Slav blood inside me started to boil.

Today, my office feels like a prison—the walls are closing in on me more than usual. I know it's in my head, but I still hate it.

Logan managed to get me a secure communication channel, and starting today, I should be meeting my girlfriends online for the next five days.

My laptop chimes as the first participant enters my Zoom call.

"Hello, Maisy!" Georgina's face fills my screen, her perfect white teeth bared in an amazing smile. This woman could sell million-dollar properties on her worst day. "How are you holding up?"

I smile back. "I'm good, thanks. You?"

"Still feeling awful for caving, honestly."

"Oh, stop it," I say, waving it off. "Anyone would've done the same, especially knowing how crude and ruthless Orion, Logan, and Kai can be."

Before Georgina can respond, the screen splits—

Angelina joins the call.

"Maisy." She nods at me, then at Georgina. "Good to see you both."

Celina pops in next, her cropped hair visible even in the small Zoom window. "Sorry I'm late," she says, adjusting her camera. "Lost track of time at the dojo."

The final box fills with Gizelle's face, her chandelier earrings catching the light as she settles in her chair. She always wears fancy jewelry straight from Italy. "Ciao tutti."

"Thanks for joining today," I begin. "Leila and Sasha won't be joining us. They're here at the house, helping me with a few things. And honestly, I wanted to keep this call smaller. What I need to discuss is sensitive."

Celina leans forward. "Is everything okay?"

"I was wondering why you wanted to meet via Zoom," Gizelle says, sounding concerned.

"Well, for starters, I won't be able to leave my house for the next five days. For security reasons."

"What? They can't do that to you!" Georgina snaps. She and Gizelle wear the same expression—stunned disbelief. Of course, Angelina and Celina are fully aware of what's happening.

"It's okay, Georgina. I agreed to it. And it's fine."

"What's happening in five days?" Gizelle asks.

"The Mafia Council is meeting to decide if Viktor will be given the Slavs' quarter of New York."

"Do you think there's a chance he'll get it?" Angelina asks.

"That's what I want your help with. We found out that Viktor's been smuggling people. In shipping containers." The words taste bitter in my mouth. "And we know how the mafia feels about human trafficking."

The faces on my screen harden.

"I know about one shipment so far," I continue. "But I need evidence. Hard evidence that ties him directly to the operation. Documents, manifests, financial trails, surveillance footage—anything that proves he's responsible."

Gizelle is already typing something on her phone. "My cousins have connections at the Port Authority of New York. If any containers arrived there…"

"I can check the real estate angle," Georgina says. "Storage facilities, warehouse purchases. I have access to property records that aren't public yet."

Celina nods. "I train with two police officers. They owe me favors."

"My sister-in-law might know something," Angelina says quietly. "She works for the FBI and they hear things, especially about newcomers trying to establish territory."

"I need this to stick," I say firmly. "How we

handle Viktor...it sets the stage for everything that comes next."

Gizelle's still typing furiously. "I'm already accessing shipping manifests through my import contacts. Cross-referencing with customs declarations."

"Angelina, can you get CCTV footage from the docks?" I ask.

She nods. "I have a contact in security. I'll call him right after this."

"I need physical evidence delivered here," I tell them. "Nothing digital that can be traced back to any of you."

"I'll coordinate the couriers," Georgina offers. "I have real estate clients coming and going all the time. No one will notice a few extra messengers."

My mind is already racing ahead, anticipating problems. "Be careful," I warn them.

"Maisy?" Angelina's voice pulls me back. "We've got this. Really."

I nod, grateful and guilty both at once that they would put themselves at risk. "Thank you."

"Already found something," Gizelle interjects, eyes fixed on something off-screen. "A container that arrived three days ago. Manifested as furniture from North Macedonia, but the weight was off by about 1,500 pounds."

"Bingo," I whisper.

"The receiver is listed as Mrozovski Imports," she continues, "but I'm looking at customs forms with a different company name. Documentation doesn't match."

"That's a start."

Celina's face is grim. "My police contacts can pull arrest records for trafficking suspects. See if any of them included Viktor before they mysteriously went silent."

"Or disappeared entirely," Georgina adds.

I sigh. "I got five days to build a case against Viktor."

"I'll start compiling what we find," Angelina says. "Create a physical dossier with copies of everything."

"Perfect." I nod. "So, same time tomorrow?"

They all agree, and one by one, their faces disappear from my screen, leaving me alone in my home office once more.

I rest my hands on my desk, feeling the cool wood beneath my palms, anchoring myself to something solid while my mind races.

Viktor Mrozovski doesn't understand what I am. What I've survived.

DAY 2

MAISY

The package arrives just after noon, an innocuous manila envelope delivered by a courier who left it in the hands of one of the men guarding our house. I know instantly what it contains. I close the door and carry it to my office.

Inside, I find a thick, meticulously organized folder—shipping manifests with highlighted discrepancies. Financial records showing shell companies. CCTV stills of Viktor's men at the docks. Witness statements collected by Celina's police contacts. And photographs—God, the photographs—of people emerging from containers, disoriented and desperate.

I spread the evidence across my desk, my

photographic memory cataloguing each detail. Viktor Mrozovski's human trafficking operation is laid bare.

I take out my phone and send a simple text to Orion, Logan, and Kai: My office. Now.

They arrive within minutes—Orion first, instantly studying my expression to assess my mood. Logan follows behind him, and Kai comes last, his eyes looking electric with curiosity.

"I've got something," I tell them, gesturing over the spread of documents.

Orion steps forward first, picking up the shipping manifest. His eyebrows rise slightly—the closest he ever comes to showing surprise. "Viktor's operation."

"All of it," I confirm, watching as Logan and Kai move to examine different documents.

"Jesus," Logan whispers, focusing on the photos of the trafficked people. "Some of these individuals show signs of severe dehydration, possible hypoxia..."

Kai snatches up a financial document. "These are transactions through one of his shell companies. How the hell did you get these?"

I don't answer directly. Some secrets stay mine. "I had help."

Orion looks up from the custody chain documents he's examining, his expression careful. "Maisy, you didn't have to do this. We've been gathering evidence as well."

Something flares in my chest—irritation, perhaps, or the old fear of being sidelined. "How far along are you?"

Logan glances at Orion, then back at me. "Not as far as you, sweetheart. These financial trails—we were still trying to crack his offshore accounts."

"Well then," I say, unable to keep the satisfaction from my voice, "it's good that I did this."

Kai grins, that wild expression that reminds me why I fell for him despite myself. "Baby girl, you've got Viktor by the balls with this."

"The Council will not ignore Viktor's activities," Orion says. "Especially with children involved." He taps a document showing the ages of the trafficked individuals.

Logan points to one of the shipping routes. "This proves a systematic operation. Not just a one-off mistake by an underling he can disavow."

"The brothers are involved too," Kai points out, holding up a surveillance photo showing Viktor's brothers overseeing a container being loaded. "Family business."

Orion starts putting the documents back into the folder. His legal mind is already organizing a case. "This is exactly what we needed. We got four days to prepare our presentation to the Council."

"And then?" I ask, though I know the answer.

"And then Viktor loses everything," Logan says softly, the threat in his gentle voice all the more chilling for its quietness.

Kai cracks his knuckles. "Including his life, if I have anything to say about it."

"One step at a time," Orion cautions. "First, we secure New York. Then, we decide how Viktor pays."

My brain can't help calculating the odds. The Council meeting is still three days away. Viktor could discover what we're doing. He could strike first.

"This is solid," Logan assures me, professional assessment in his tone. "Ironclad. Viktor won't wriggle out of this."

Kai is still looking at the photos of the trafficked people, unusual solemnity on his face. "These could've been any of us, you know? In another life."

It could've been me, I think, but don't say. In this life.

"We should go," Orion says finally, tucking the folder under his arm. "There's work to be done before the Council meeting." He leans down, pressing a kiss to my lips. "Thank you, darling. This was...unexpected, but perfect."

Logan follows suit, his kiss landing on my cheek. "Let us handle things from here."

Kai's last, as always, pulling me into a full-on embrace that lifts me slightly off my feet. "My clever baby girl," he murmurs against my hair. "Always surprising us."

They take the evidence with them and leave me alone in my office once more.

I walk to the window, looking out at the slice of New York that belongs to us—to me. The satisfaction I felt moments ago turns into something bitter. They took the folder—my work, my connections, my risk—and just...left. Off to plan without me. Again.

My fingers curl into fists against the windowsill. After everything, they still see me as something to be protected rather than someone to be included. I managed to get what they couldn't. Yet when it comes to the next steps, they close ranks and leave me behind.

"Let us handle things from here," Logan said. As if I haven't been handling things all along.

I press my forehead against the cool glass, the frustration burning in my chest, familiar yet unwelcome. A genius mind trapped in a gilded cage—what good is that? While they meet and strategize, I'm left here with nothing but my thoughts.

Three more days of this. Three more days of being sidelined in my own fight.

DAY 3

MAISY

My screen glows blue in the darkness of my office, the only light source in the room. I check the time: 9:00 PM. I should be putting my children to bed right now, but I asked Orion to do that tonight.

I have something to take care of.

Georgina should be calling any minute. This time, she's the only one I've invited. Some conversations require fewer witnesses.

My fingers tap against the desk in anticipation of the computer chiming. And there it is. It's Georgina's calling.

I accept, and her face fills my screen.

"Hey, Maisy." Her voice is softer than usual.

"Georgina." I offer a small smile, eyes flicking to the corners of her screen, analyzing the background. She's somewhere private. Good. "Thanks for doing this."

"I'll do anything to make it up to you." She leans closer to her camera, concern etched across her features. "Saying that, are you sure—"

I cut her off. "I'm sure." I made that decision

yesterday, when they walked out with my evidence, leaving me behind. Again. "Did you speak to him?"

She nods, glancing over her shoulder. "He's here."

My heart rate accelerates. "Let's not waste time then."

Georgina disappears briefly, the screen showing only her empty chair. My memory flashes to yesterday—Orion taking the folder, Logan telling me to rest, Kai's kiss to my hair. All of them walking away to plan my future without me.

The screen shifts, and Viktor Mrozovski appears.

His presence commands attention, even through a digital interface. Dark hair slicked back, sharp features set in a mask of controlled interest. His ice-pale eyes study me with predatory focus. He wears a tailored suit despite the late hour. Dark blue.

He chuckles. "I must admit, your message was...unexpected."

I straighten my spine, meeting his gaze directly. "I imagine it was," I reply. "But necessary."

"You want to switch sides." He raises one eyebrow, his skepticism evident. "Betray your men and join me instead. Forgive me if I find that difficult to believe. Especially when you ran away from my house."

I laugh, the sound hollow even to my own ears. "Is it really that hard to believe? Look around, Viktor." I gesture to my surroundings. "I'm trapped in my own home while they make decisions about my territory. My life. And just to clarify, I didn't run from your house. I was drugged. Kidnapped. Maybe you should worry less about my loyalty and more about your security."

Something flickers in his eyes—interest, perhaps. Or recognition.

"I've been sidelined my entire life," I continue, the words flowing from a place of genuine frustration. "First by Milan the Dog, then by the men who claimed to love me. I'm tired of being protected instead of respected."

Viktor leans back slightly. "And what makes you think I would respect you?"

"Because you need me." I let the truth ring clear. "You want my territory, but the Council won't just hand it to you. With me standing beside you, your claim becomes legitimate."

His eyes narrow. "A convenient arrangement for you."

"For both of us." I lean closer to the camera, letting him see the determination in my eyes. "I know about your human trafficking operation. So do Orion, Logan, and Kai."

His face hardens into stone, but I press on before he can speak.

"They have evidence. Concrete evidence that will

destroy you at the Council meeting." I pause, letting him process the threat. "Unless I help you."

His voice drops lower. "And why would you do that?"

"Because I want out." The conviction in my voice surprises even me. "I want my freedom. I want to be seen as more than a prize to be protected."

Viktor studies me for a long moment, his gaze dissecting. I've seen that look before—men trying to find the weakness, the angle, the lie. I don't blink.

"Words are easy, Maisy," he finally says. "Proof is more convincing."

I nod. "I thought you might say that. That's why I sent a gesture of goodwill."

Georgina reappears beside Viktor, holding a thick folder—identical to the one my men took yesterday. She places it on the table in front of him.

"Everything they have on you," I explain as Viktor opens the folder. "Shipping manifests. Financial records. Witness statements. Photos. All the evidence they planned to present to the Council."

Viktor flips through the documents, his face unreadable. Behind him, two familiar men move into frame—his brothers. They peer over his shoulder at the papers, eyes widening.

"It's all here," one brother says. "Everything."

The other brother, Igor, looks directly at the

camera, at me. "Welcome to the family, Maisy."

Viktor closes the folder slowly, deliberately. When he looks up, something has changed in his eyes. The ice has thawed just enough to reveal calculation behind it. "This is...comprehensive." His fingers tap the folder.

"Thank you," I say simply.

Viktor's lips curve into what might almost be a smile. "And what exactly do you want in return?"

"I want to be there," I say firmly. "At the Council meeting. Standing beside you when my men walk in. I want them to see exactly what they've lost by underestimating me."

He considers this, head tilted slightly. "And after?"

"After, I want my children brought to me. And a new life, away from New York." The lie comes easily, wrapped in enough truth to be believable.

Viktor studies me for another long moment before nodding. "I believe we can accommodate that."

His brother leans forward. "This is a cause for celebration, brother."

"Indeed." Viktor's eyes never leave mine. "Maisy Roy, you've made a wise decision today. One that will be rewarded."

Georgina steps back into frame. "Viktor would like you to have this." She holds up a cellphone. "For direct communication."

"Your friend will have it delivered to you first thing tomorrow," Viktor says. "There are details we should discuss privately before the Council meeting."

My heart rate spikes again, but I keep my expression neutral. "I look forward to it."

"As do I." Something like hunger flashes across his face. "In two days, we will stand before the Council together. And your men will learn what happens when they fail to value what they have."

His brothers murmur agreement behind him.

"Two days," I confirm, forcing a smile that I know doesn't reach my eyes.

"Until then." Viktor inclines his head slightly, a gesture that might be respect. Then the screen goes black as he disconnects.

I sit in the sudden darkness of my office, heart pounding in my ears. What I've just done—the risk I've taken—settles over me like a heavy cloak.

I think of the plan I've made, and that it's now set in motion.

My computer rings again and it's Georgina, now calling from her car.

"It's done," I say quietly.

She nods. "He believed every word. So did his brothers."

"And the other part?"

"In progress." Georgina's eyes meet mine. "Maisy, are you absolutely sure about this? If they find out..."

"They won't. Not until it's too late."

She studies me for a moment longer, then nods. "I'll let the others know phase one is complete."

DAY 4

MAISY

The courier arrives just after lunch, and one of the armed men standing outside the house signs for it. I collect the package, a small brown box with Viktor's burner inside, I presume, and head to my office.

I quickly open the box to make sure it's the cell. I smile upon seeing it, my fingers curling around it, feeling its weight. A tangible connection to the enemy. I check that my office door is locked before powering it on.

No contacts. No history. Just a blank slate waiting for my betrayal to begin.

I don't waste time. I type:

Need to warn you. Overheard Orion, Logan, and Kai planning. They intend to attack if the Council rules against them. Bringing all their men.

I hit send before I can second-guess myself. The phone feels hot in my palm, burning with consequences. My heart hammers against my ribs while I wait for his response.

The reply comes fast:

Expected as much. We'll be prepared.

I take a deep breath and push further:

How many men do you have? I might be able to help.

Three dots appear, disappear, appear again. He's measuring his response, weighing up how much to reveal.

44 total. My brothers and I have been recruiting.

I smile to myself. Perfect. My fingers dance across the screen:

I can bring the women from my club. No one will risk opening fire if their wives and daughters are present. They'll be excellent shields.

This time, his response is immediate:

Clever girl. Bring everyone you can.

I power down the phone and slip it into my desk drawer, underneath a stack of the children's artwork.

The rest of the day I spend in careful preparation, making calls through secure lines, organizing the pieces on my mental chessboard. By evening, I'm exhausted but satisfied. Tomorrow's

Council meeting will change everything—one way or another.

It's late in the evening, just after I've put the children to bed, when Orion, Logan, and Kai come home. I hear three sets of footsteps—heavy, purposeful, familiar—approaching my office. The door is open and they regard me.

"You're still up," Orion observes.

"Couldn't sleep," I reply, leaning back in my chair. "Big day tomorrow."

Logan circles the desk, perching on the edge beside where I sit. "That's actually why we're here. We wanted to talk about tomorrow."

"The Council meeting," Kai clarifies, unnecessarily.

I look between the three of them, these dangerous men who think they own me. I keep my voice neutral. "What about it?"

Orion takes the chair opposite mine, his dark eyes intent. "We'll be leaving early in the morning. The meeting's set for noon, but we wanna ensure everything's secured beforehand."

"We've arranged twenty men at all entry points," Logan adds, his gentle voice at odds with his words. "Another fifteen inside. Viktor won't be able to make a move without us knowing."

Kai flashes a grin that doesn't reach his eyes.

"And if he tries anything, we'll be ready."

"We've prepared our presentation of the evidence," Orion continues. No doubt his lawyer's mind has run through every argument and counter-argument. "The Council can't ignore human trafficking."

"What do you think Viktor will do when he loses?" I ask, genuinely curious about their assessment.

The three exchange glances.

"He'll either accept the Council's ruling," Logan says slowly, "or..."

"Or he'll try something stupid," Kai finishes, cracking his knuckles.

"Either way," Orion says with finality, "we'll handle it. You don't need to worry about anything."

There it is again. The dismissal. The sidelining. We'll handle it. You don't need to worry.

"I understand," I say, smiling slightly. "You've got it all worked out."

"We just wanted you to know everything's under control," Logan says, his hand moving to my shoulder in what's meant to be reassurance.

"Sounds like you've thought of everything," I say, impressed by how calm my voice remains.

"That's the plan, baby girl," Kai says. "This time tomorrow, Viktor Mrozovski will be finished in New York."

If only they knew.

"I'm not worried," I tell them, meeting each pair of eyes in turn. "You've got it in hand." I pause, letting my smile widen. "And so do I."

Orion's gaze sharpens. "What does that mean?"

I shrug casually. "Just that I trust you to handle things." The lie slips out smooth as silk. "I know tomorrow will go exactly as it should."

He studies me for a moment longer. Finally, he nods, apparently satisfied. "Come on, let's get some rest, darling. Tomorrow will be a long day for all of us."

Logan leans down to press a kiss to my lips. "Everything will be fine, sweetheart. I promise."

Kai pulls me from my chair and into his arms. "This time tomorrow, it's over. Then we can get back to normal."

Normal. As if there's ever been such a thing in my life.

DAY 5

ORION

We arrive at the Council meeting exactly forty-five minutes early, although we've been out since the morning. It's a point of principle—control the room before anyone else can claim it. Logan and Kai flank me as we enter the bare, cavernous hall with its concrete walls and industrial lighting. The massive round table at the center is a statement in itself.

The evidence sits inside my briefcase. I've built an airtight case against Viktor. And I'm ready.

I check my watch and glance around. Our men are already in position throughout the building.

Logan catches my eye. "Everything ready?"

I nod. "Perfect." And it is. We've planned for every contingency.

The other families file in gradually, their faces a study in politics and power. They take their seats, each flanked by associates.

At noon precisely, Gallo, the Council head, calls the meeting to order. "Gentlemen, we're here to address the petition filed by Viktor Mrozovski regarding the Slavic quarter of New York City."

Everyone looks at the four empty chairs at the table, the chairs Viktor and his brothers should be occupying by now.

Seeing that they're not here yet, all eyes shift to me—to us. The unspoken question hangs in the air: did we steal that territory? The answer is complicated. We claimed it after its previous leadership collapsed. Made it profitable. Protected it.

"Mr. Mrozovski appears to be delayed," Gallo continues, checking his watch. "In the meantime, Mr. Carte, I understand you have evidence to present?"

I stand, unbuttoning my suit jacket. "Indeed." I extract the folder from my briefcase, passing it to Gallo. "Evidence of Viktor Mrozovski's human trafficking operation."

A ripple of discomfort passes through the room. Gallo's face hardens as he examines the first document. He passes the folder to the man beside him, who studies it before passing it along. The evidence travels around the table, expressions darkening with each new pair of eyes that sees it.

"This is…substantial," Gallo admits when the folder returns to him. "And disturbing."

I allow myself a moment of satisfaction. "Viktor Mrozovski is not fit to control any territory in this city."

Twenty minutes into the meeting, Gallo checks his watch again. "Given Mr. Mrozovski's continued absence and the evidence presented, I suggest we rule—"

The double doors at the far end of the hall swing open with deliberate force.

For fuck's sake.

Is that…is that Maisy?

Fitted black three-piece suit, black tie, six-inch heels, hair pulled back, makeup on her face, red lips, powerful stance.

I narrow my eyes to make sure I'm seeing right, then glance at Kai and Logan. Their raised eyebrows tell me everything.

She strides into the room, with her friends by her side—Georgina, Celina, and Angelina.

"Gentlemen." Maisy's voice is deeper than usual.

She approaches Viktor's empty place at the table. Celina removes three of the four chairs, leaving only one, which Maisy takes like it's a throne.

Rage and confusion war within me. What game is she playing? Who is this woman wearing my wife's face?

"Maisy, what are you doing?" Kai hisses through clenched teeth, the question I can't bring myself to ask.

She ignores him completely, surveying the room with those dark eyes that miss nothing.

Gallo recovers first. "We were expecting Mr. Mrozovski and his brothers for the matter concerning the Slavic territory, Miss...?"

"Maisy. Maisy Slavinovich." Her smile is chilling. "Mr. Mrozovski sends his regrets. He won't be joining us." She makes a pause, perfectly timed. "None of them will."

A ripple of alarm rolls through the room. Gallo straightens in his chair, his tone sharper now. "Are you suggesting what I think you are?"

Maisy tilts her head slightly. "I'm not suggesting anything. I'm informing you."

My fingers clamp down on the table edge, iron-tight, like I could crush the wood beneath my grip. My knuckles burn white, the pressure humming up my arms. I can't speak. Can't breathe. What I'm seeing—this—it's so far beyond what should even be possible, and for the first time, I'm speechless.

Logan's still processing, I see it in his eyes. Kai looks ready to vault across the table, though whether to confront her or protect her, I'm not sure.

"Gentlemen," Maisy says again, commanding the room with authority, "I have gifts for all of you."

She nods toward the doors. Four women enter, each carrying a white cake box tied with black ribbon. They place them at intervals around the table.

Salvatore Esposito, old-school to the core, laughs harshly. "You brought cake? Rightly so—the kitchen is where your place is, woman."

Several men join him in laughter.

"Open them," she commands.

The women move in perfect synchronization, untying ribbons, lifting lids. The laughter dies instantly, replaced by gasps and curses.

Four severed heads. Viktor and his brothers, their expressions frozen in permanent shock. Their slicked-back hair still perfect, their dead eyes staring at nothing.

She's become ruthless, untamed—so far beyond my control it feels like the ground beneath me is tilting, daring me to maintain my footing. My brilliant, merciless wife just executed four men and delivered their heads to the most powerful criminal organization.

Esposito half-rises from his chair. "You assassinated the Mrozovski brothers without sanction?" His voice cuts through the room like a blade. "That's a declaration of war."

She smiles again, wolfish this time. "You mean like the war he started when he trafficked people across borders and tried to wipe out my bloodline? Tell me,

Salvatore, how long did you know about his operation? Months? Years?"

The accusation hangs in the air, venomous and precise.

"I had no knowledge—"

"Don't lie to me." Maisy's voice turns lethal. "Not in front of these men."

A few heads turn uncomfortably. The silence that follows is cold and unforgiving.

Gallo leans forward, choosing his words carefully. "Even with the crimes outlined, execution without trial, delivering heads in cake boxes…This Council has rules. You're not above them."

"Neither was Viktor. Yet none of you stopped him. I did."

Another voice pipes up, this time from a young and ambitious Italian whose name escapes me. "If you did this, how can we be sure you won't do the same to one of us next time you feel slighted?"

He freezes when Maisy's gaze pierces him like a scalpel. "Because I don't act on feelings. I act on evidence. Of betrayal. Of threats to my people. If you're not guilty of any of those things, you have nothing to fear."

Then, without flinching, she adds, "But if you are…fear would be wise."

The room stills.

Maisy lets the weight of her words settle before adding, quieter, more intimate, yet no less deadly: "You want to question my methods? Fine. Question them. But also ask yourselves this—why did it take a woman in heels, with a bloodstained name, to do what none of you had the balls to?"

The sting lands. No one speaks. Some avert their eyes.

She straightens and gestures toward the folder. "You've already seen the evidence against Viktor. You know he deserved what he got."

Behind her, the doors open again. Women pour in—dozens, then hundreds. I recognize some of them. Wives, daughters, girlfriends, secretaries. They line the walls of the hall, their expressions unified in purpose.

Gallo attempts to regain control. "Miss Slavinovich, while we appreciate your initiative, this Council exists to maintain order and prevent exactly this kind of—"

"Now," she interrupts—interrupts the head of the Council, something even I would hesitate to do. "Take a good look at my associates." She gestures to the women surrounding us. "Together, we have something on each and every one of you. We are a network that can never be broken, all thanks to you."

"What do you want?" Esposito demands, his earlier mockery replaced by poorly concealed fear.

Maisy's smile widens. "Absolutely nothing."

Confusion spreads around the table.

"I just came here so you all could meet me," she explains, "and to pass on the message that Maisy the Slav lives. The Cartes, Vitalis, Delgados, and Slavs have owned New York for years, and that's how it's going to stay."

Her eyes finally find mine. What I feel for her in that moment is complex beyond words. Fury at her deception. Admiration for her audacity. Hurt that she kept such secrets. Pride in her brilliance. And something deeper, something that burns hotter than before—the recognition that the woman I thought I knew is even more extraordinary than I imagined.

"The territory is mine," she states, addressing the entire Council. "I speak for it. I decide its fate. Me."

One by one, the family heads begin to pound their fists against the table—the traditional sign of acknowledgment and respect. Not all of them are thrilled, but the ritual holds. I find my own fist joining them, the silver rings on my fingers striking the wood in rhythm with the others. Logan and Kai follow. The sound builds like a heartbeat, like thunder, echoing off the concrete walls.

Maisy waits for silence before giving a single, crisp nod. "This meeting is concluded."

She turns from the table, her women forming a

protective formation around her as she walks back toward the doors. As she passes our seats, she pauses briefly, looking at Kai, Logan, and me in turn.

She offers the slightest incline of her head—an acknowledgment between equals, perhaps for the first time.

Then she's leaving, striding through the doors, her army of women flowing out with her like water.

The Council room erupts into chaos the moment she's gone—some of the men are arguing, questioning, demanding answers. I ignore them all, rising from my seat without hesitation. Logan and Kai follow my lead immediately.

We exit without talking to anyone, moving with purpose down the corridor. I spot her leaning briefly against a wall, looking vulnerable for a moment, though it is quickly masked when Georgina approaches her. This is the woman I married—steel and softness in equal measure, a complexity I'm only now beginning to fully appreciate.

"Give us room," she tells Georgina and the other women when she sees us. They hesitate, then retreat, leaving just the four of us in the corridor.

I stop a few feet from her.

"You could've told us."

Her response is immediate, confident. "Would you have let me handle it my way?"

No. I wouldn't have. We both know it.

"You killed them," Logan says quietly.

"They threatened my family. You do that, you die," she replies simply.

Kai steps forward first, closing the distance between them. "You outplayed everyone in that room."

A ghost of a smile touches her lips. "That was the point."

"You've rewritten the rules of the game today," I say.

"Good," she says. "The old rules never favored women anyway."

Logan laughs. "And you brought an army to a Council meeting."

"I brought a reminder," she corrects him, "that power doesn't always look the way men expect it to."

Kai lifts her off her feet in an embrace that would crush a lesser woman. "My fierce, beautiful, terrifying baby girl."

"I don't know what you did or how you did it," I say finally, as we stand in the empty corridor, "but it's time we stopped underestimating you." I take her hand. "You, Maisy, have the blood of a mafia head running through your veins. I would be honored to rule alongside you."

"Me too," Logan says, stepping forward, his eyes filled with newfound respect.

"Damn right, me too," Kai adds, unable to contain the fierce pride in his voice.

Maisy looks between us, something shifting in her expression—a wall coming down, perhaps. "I can't promise I'll always be the head of the Slavs unless it's needed. But now we have more of us at the Council table."

"A united front," I murmur, the strategic implications already unfurling in my mind.

"You cut off their heads?" Kai asks in disbelief, his tone caught between horror and admiration. "How?"

She gives us a smile that sends a chill down my spine—the smile of a woman who always sees more than she reveals. "It wasn't me. It was my network. We know people who know people who kill people." She shrugs, the gesture deceptively casual. "And we have something on everyone."

The implications of her words settle over us—the scope of her influence, the depth of her planning.

"If I didn't know you," Logan says, shaking his head slowly, "I'd say you're fucking scary, Maisy."

Her laughter echoes softly around the corridor. "You don't know me yet. Not completely." She runs her hand over the side of her head, as if to check her hair remains perfect. Her dark eyes meet mine with an intensity that makes my breath catch. "But you will."

The promise in her words ignites something

within me. This isn't about control anymore. It's about standing beside a woman whose brilliance and ruthlessness match my own. Perhaps exceed them. I'm facing an equal, and the revelation doesn't threaten me—it exhilarates me.

What flows between us in this moment isn't just respect or desire—it's the foundation of something I've never truly experienced with a woman before: genuine partnership.

"Lead the way, darling," I tell her, offering my arm. "It seems you always have."

THE END

From betrayal to bloodshed, from lust to love - you stayed with Maisy and her men to the very end.

If you've made it this far, you're part of my world now.

And I'd love to stay connected.

Join my newsletter (via my website) to get early sneak peeks of my next love-obsessed, rule-breaking stories.. maybe even before anyone else does.

With all my love,
Alexandra